Tongue-tied, Cory sat down on the bed and began stripping off her shoes, socks, and jeans. Desperately wanting something to cover her seminakedness, she crawled beneath the covers.

When Julia joined her, Cory's anxiety mounted. The other woman was completely naked.

Julia smiled as she toyed with the collar of Cory's shirt.

"You're a rather shy one, aren't you?" Julia was keenly aware of the awkwardness of the situation. It didn't usually go like this. Women usually fell hungrily into her arms . . .

Dammit. She felt like she was practically forcing herself on the woman.

LOOKING FOR NAIAD?

CHANGE OF

Heart

A novel by
LINDA HILL

CHANGE OF

A novel by

LINDA HILL

THE NAIAD PRESS, INC.
1999

Printed in the United States of America on acid-free paper
First Edition

Editor: Lila Empson
Cover designer: Bonnie Liss (Phoenix Graphics)
Typesetter: Sandi Stancil

Library of Congress Cataloging-in-Publication Data

Hill, Linda, 1958 –
    Change of heart / by Linda Hill.
        p.   cm.
    ISBN 1-56280-238-0   (alk. paper)
    I. Title.
PS3558.I392C48   1999
813'.54—dc21   98-46296
                                                                        CIP

For Kate

Acknowledgments

Many thanks to the women who work so hard to make these books happen, including Sandi Stancil, Bonnie Liss, Kathleen DeBold, and Lila Empson.

My thanks to the women at Naiad, particularly Barbara and Donna for their trust, and to Charity and Alex for their sweetness.

A long overdue thanks to Jenny-Jenny. Much love and thanks to my family — who have given me such love and support for so many years — my sister Dani, Rob, Anissa, and Angie. *(Ain't Nobody!)* Thanks to Anita for holding down the fort, and as always to Judy, Barb, Cheryl, and Debra.

Finally, thanks to Bonnie and to my dad — who somehow still manages to believe his daughter is something special.

About the Author

Linda Hill is living happily-ever-after near Boston with her partner of ten years and their two pups, Molly and Maggie. Her previous novels include *Never Say Never, Class Reunion,* and *Just Yesterday.* Her short stories have appeared in several Naiad anthologies, including *Dancing in the Dark, Lady Be Good,* and *The Touch of Your Hand.*

CHANGE OF

Heart

A novel by
LINDA HILL

Chapter 1

Julia Westgate drew the damp towel away from her hair and lifted it to the mirror. Slowly, she rubbed the towel against the surface of the steam-covered glass until her image began to materialize.

Unsmiling, she brought the towel back and rubbed her hair vigorously before dropping the towel on the floor.

Not bad, she thought, leaning forward to eye the results in the mirror. *Color in a bottle. Washes out in twenty days.* She pushed slender fingers through the damp curls, liking the way the light caught it. She'd never gone this dark before. Her hair was nearly black, the perfect color for the short cut she'd sat through only an hour earlier.

Next she examined the color of her near-perfect brows. Her eyes darted from the brows to the top of her head. She nodded, satisfied.

She picked up a bottle of styling lotion and poured a dollop the size of a nickel in the palm of her left hand. She rubbed the lotion between her palms before running her fingers along her scalp and letting her fingertips slip through the curls, lifting them into place. She would let her hair dry just like that, she decided, then grinned as she thought of Raymond.

He would be furious. She could hear the sound of his tsk-tsking, as if as he were standing right behind her. He would be so exasperated with what she'd done to her long curls that he would punish her mercilessly by making her wear wigs until long after her hair and its color had grown out.

A high price to pay, she knew, but she'd weighed it out heavily before keeping her appointment at the salon on Newbury Street. The shoot had run much longer than expected, and she'd nearly had to cancel. But seeing the results of the cut and color, she was glad that she'd had the cabby drive like a maniac to get her to the appointment. It had definitely been worth it. She only hoped she'd feel the same way at the end of the evening.

How long had it been, anyway? Nearly two years, she was certain. Oh, there had been the night in France about eight months ago that had turned into a complete fiasco. She'd been recognized before she got inside the door of the club. She'd lied, of course, and told the admirer that she didn't know who Julia

Westgate was. But the encounter had left her too shaken even to step inside the bar.

It was different here, in the states, she told herself. No one here gave a hoot about European fashion models. People were all too bloody wrapped up in their Washington politics and Hollywood movie stars to give two shakes about what was going on across the ocean. Especially about some fashion model. Not like in Europe, where they treated their models like celebrities. Like royalty.

She inspected her features, satisfied with her new look. Without makeup, the sprinkle of freckles that crossed the bridge of her nose and spilled onto her high cheekbones stood out. They were the light reddish-brown color often found on the features of someone with Irish blood. Her mother's genes. Natural auburn hair and milk-white skin.

She stared into the reflection of her dark amethyst eyes before allowing her gaze to wander over her other features.

She wasn't certain, but she didn't think anyone could possibly recognize her. She smiled a bit, then scoffed when she caught sight of the creases around her eyes.

Damn, I'm getting old. Not that thirty-eight was really old. She rather liked knowing that her twenties were well behind her, and she didn't really mind the new wrinkles. But Raymond minded. The camera minded. There were all kinds of tricks played with photographs to brush away the signs of age. But there was no way to hide the lines under the harsh lights of the modeling runways.

"Don't smile," Raymond barked. "Show no facial expression."

It exhausted her to think about Raymond now, and of the career that was fading. *Too old. You look too old. Advertisers want fresh, young faces.*

She clamped her mind shut to the thoughts. "Not tonight," she told her reflection. "I won't let you in tonight." She tilted her head to one side and thought about the evening ahead. "Tonight is for me." She allowed a quick smile and stepped over the discarded towel on her way to the bedroom.

She already knew what she would wear. Tight black jeans tucked into slender boots. Not those heavy boots that the young ones were wearing these days. These were sleek. Fashionable. Tasteful. A simple cotton sweater. A cream-color creation that gave away the angles of her shoulders without clinging. And a leather jacket. Simple. Straight lines. She looked tall. Angular. Slender.

Chapter 2

Stifling a yawn, Cory Hayes lifted one knee and planted her foot flat on the wall behind her. She leaned back, lounging against the cool tile, and tried not to look at her watch one more time.

She glanced around at the tables in the café, doing a quick check to make sure that none of her tables needed anything. Only three of the tables were occupied. A lesbian couple whispered intimately over coffee. Two gay men sat a few feet away, barely speaking to each other. The last table was filled with six men, laughing raucously while they drank more than they ate.

Cory checked her watch and silently groaned. Eight o'clock. Just one more hour before her shift was over. One more hour before her friends would start arriving.

She didn't usually mind filling in for Jeff when one of his wait staff wanted to take an evening off. The money was good, and the *Tribune* was barely paying enough to cover her rent. But she wished for the umpteenth time in the last six hours that she'd never committed to this night.

When she'd said yes, she hadn't known that the day would be a special one. She didn't know that, after two years of sweating in the copy room rewriting newspaper copy for the regular beat writers, today would finally be the day her sweat paid off.

An anonymous lead had come in about a week ago. A phone call from an elderly woman who complained about the dogs that barked incessantly next door. None of the reporters wanted to bother checking it out, so one night after work Cory had wandered down to the address that the woman had left. What she found horrified her. About a dozen dogs and nearly two dozen puppies, unkempt and ungroomed, were pressed into tiny wire crates barely big enough for them to stand up.

The man who owned the dogs was breeding them in the worst conditions imaginable, and Cory set out to write an article that would gain the attention of city officials and anyone else who might be able to do something about the mistreatment.

Her plan had already worked. As part of her investigation, she had contacted many of the animal shelters and animal rights groups, and they had already been taken action. They had removed the dogs from the horrible conditions and placed them in a kennel. Cory had even helped out with the bathing and grooming. Many of the dogs were shy, and they cowered when she came near them. By the time she'd finished her story, she was both bewildered and angered by the mistreatment and abuse that the dogs had endured.

The article she'd written highlighted the abuse of the animals and their subsequent rescue. But the focus of the article was to generate enough interest from caring people who would hopefully go down to the shelter and adopt the dogs.

"It's almost a fluff piece," her boss, Edgar, had growled. "But I hate people who treat animals like shit." He only gave her the briefest of nods. "We'll run it tonight. Page three." His wave was nonchalant, but Cory knew that he was aware of just how much this chance meant to her.

"You've got somebody waiting at table four." Randy, the maître d', gave her a wink as he made his way toward the bar. "Thought I'd do you a little favor."

Caught daydreaming, Cory snapped to attention and edged her way toward her left until she could get a glimpse around the column that blocked her view of table four.

"Hmm." She hid the smile that pulled at the corners of her mouth. *A favor indeed.* She couldn't see the face of the woman that sat with her back toward the kitchen. But under the soft lights, Cory could see short black curls just reaching the nape of a long, white neck. A camel-color sweater covered straight, sharply angled shoulders. As Cory approached, the woman's dark head slowly bent and then lifted as her slender hand turned a page of the menu.

Cory brushed just past the table and turned to stand beside the empty chair at the table for two.

The woman did not lift her head, but rather seemed to bend her head farther to give the menu her full attention.

Cory had her waitress-smile ready and tried not to grow irritated as she studied the woman. *Is she ignoring me on purpose?* Surely the woman knew she was standing less than two feet in front of her. *Great,* Cory thought, *she's a bitch.* It was inevitable, really. The gorgeous ones always were. And she *was* gorgeous. Long lashes over high cheekbones. A long, straight nose. And full, pouty lips the color of a dark rose. Even her chin was well-defined.

Cory sighed. It wasn't often that she saw a woman this striking. It was rarer still that she talked to one. And she had to talk. Now.

"Hi." The fixed smile remained on her face. Even as the dark head lifted and large wide eyes met hers.

Cory couldn't find her voice. The eyes that met hers were warm, engaging, and somewhere between the color of blue and the color of lavender. Cory had never seen such a color before.

The eyes continued to stare at her expectantly. Until slight crinkles appeared and the full lips parted.

"Hullo." The woman's voice was low and thick with a very non-American accent.

Cory came to her senses.

"Hi. My name is Cory, and I'll be serving you this evening." Somehow the words she had said so many times in the past now sounded sexual, and she felt her cheeks grow hot.

As if the woman sensed her discomfort, she raised a fine brow suggestively and replied. "How delightful." *British*, Cory thought. *Definitely British.*

"And just what will you be serving me?" Julia Westgate lowered her menu to the table and watched the color grow in Cory's cheeks. *Delightful indeed.* Her eyes swept over the slight woman before her, and a rush of adrenaline swept through her. She couldn't believe her good fortune. Cory was too perfect, too close to what she'd imagined.

Embarrassed, Cory felt a grin escape her lips. This gorgeous woman was actually flirting with her.

"Well, dinner, I suppose. Unless you'd like an appetizer first? Perhaps a drink?"

"Yes, I think so." Feeling particularly devilish, Julia checked her tongue for a split second before letting the words roll. "And perhaps dessert later on?"

Something in Cory's belly actually fluttered. "Um, sure," she faltered. "Whatever you like."

Julia watched the younger woman and gave herself a quick reprimand. Outwardly, she tilted her head to one side, looking contrite.

"Forgive me. I'm being quite naughty, aren't I?" Her accent floated around the words, making each sound like one Cory hadn't heard before.

"It's okay," Cory relaxed a bit. "You caught me off guard."

"Surely you're used to women flirting with you all the time here." Julia had selected this restaurant specifically for its reputation for fine food and gay clientele. She'd already glanced around enough to see that the bar area was filling up with women.

"Not really." Cory tried not to grimace.

"Well, I certainly find that difficult to believe." Julia's smile was captivating, the sound of her voice charming.

"I love your accent," Cory blurted. "Where are you from?"

Julia contemplated the younger woman. "Share dinner with me and I'll tell you all about it," she replied.

Cory began to stammer again, not believing for a moment that this woman could possibly find her attractive.

"Unfortunately, I'm working," she stated the obvious.

Julia frowned. "Yes, I suppose you are." Then she squinted slightly as she held Cory's gaze. "What time do you finish up?" she asked boldly.

"In about an hour."

"Perfect." Julia nodded her head, her mind made up easily. "Just in time for dessert. You *will* join me, won't you?"

"I — um." Cory thought of her friends that would be arriving shortly, of the celebration they were supposed to share. Then she stared into the striking eyes in the lovely face that tilted up to her. "Sure. Why not." *She's only kidding,* Cory thought. *An hour from now she'll have paid her bill and be long gone.*

Julia nodded. Decision made. "Great." She picked up the menu from where she'd dropped it moments before. "Now let's get down to the business of ordering, shall we? What do you recommend?"

Cory tried to hide her nervousness as she ran through the specials for the evening.

Julia finally settled on the seafood pico and watched with anticipation when Cory finally turned and walked away from her table.

She let her fingertips run along the stem of her water glass as she thought about Cory.

She couldn't have scripted the meeting any better. For a brief moment it crossed her mind that the younger woman might have a lover. Not that it mattered, really. Sometimes it was actually easier to leave a woman knowing that someone else was waiting for her. The last thing she wanted was to break some young thing's heart and leave her pining away. That had happened at least once. That she was aware of, at least. It had been back in the earlier days of her career. When she'd been reckless. Before she had learned to conceal her identity in order to keep her career safe.

Carmen had fallen for her hard. She couldn't accept that the week they'd spent together in San Francisco was the only time that they would ever share. Lovelorn, she had sent letters every day. Long letters about wanting to move to England to be with Julia. Julia had tried to ignore Carmen's pleas, but when bouquets of flowers began showing up at her doorstep, and when Raymond and the other models grew suspicious, she finally had to do something to make Carmen stop.

It had been ugly. Carmen kicked and screamed and phoned nonstop, driving Julia crazy until she broke down and asked Raymond for help. To this day, she was unclear about what Raymond had done to make Carmen stop, but she had never heard from Carmen again. She suspected that Raymond had told Carmen that he and Julia were lovers. He probably also threatened legal action of some kind, although she wasn't certain.

Raymond had only made one brief comment about the ordeal. "Look. I don't know what went on with you and that girl, but that was the first and last time that I will ever bail you out of a mess like that. If the tabloids ever got hold of a story like this, you'd be out like that." He snapped his fingers for emphasis. "You'd better learn how to keep your personal life private. Better yet, you may as well give up on having any kind of personal life as long as you're up there under the lights."

He had turned on his heel and slammed out of her dressing room, leaving her drained and shaken. She wondered how he could be so cruel, particularly since he was gay himself. But of course it didn't matter what Raymond did in his personal life. He wasn't *the product*. She was.

Enough about Raymond. She pushed thoughts of her other life away, allowing an image of Cory to slip into focus instead.

Cory had a young, fresh face with a wide, eager smile and little-boy good looks. Not that Cory was butch, Julia considered, just androgynous. Thick, dark brown hair curled over her ears and fell over her forehead. Her body appeared slight, although it was hard to tell by the way she was dressed. But Julia had noticed strong forearms beneath the rolled-up sleeves of the white shirt that she wore.

Cory wore no makeup, which Julia found refreshing. It was difficult to tell under this lighting, but she thought her eyes were green. And it was impossible to guess her age, but she was easily in her early twenties. *Robbing the cradle, eh, old girl?* Julia teased herself as she sipped at her glass of water. *And the way she blushed.* Cute, Julia decided. Cory was definitely cute.

Was it too much to hope that her luck could be this good? That the very first woman she met tonight would be the one she would spend the weekend with? She couldn't be certain. But every time her server stopped by the table to bring a new dish, pour a fresh glass of wine, and inquire about whether or not everything was to her liking, Julia grew more hopeful.

Cory was almost giddy. It was all she could do to stay focused and not get too far ahead of herself. She kept sneaking peeks at Julia throughout dinner, shaking her head, ,and disappearing in the kitchen to get a grip on her emotions. Once alone, she would convince herself that she had imagined the entire exchange, and her raging hopes and hormones would resume their normal pace. But then she would muster the courage to wander back by Julia's table, only to have her heart race when Julia let her eyelashes flutter flirtatiously.

Evelyn was the first of her friends to saunter through the front door, and Cory was on her the moment she was sure that she was out of Julia's line of vision.

"Don't be mad." Cory grabbed Evelyn by the elbow and firmly led her to a secluded table in the bar.

"Hi, sweetie." Evelyn dropped a kiss on her cheek. "Congratulations. And don't be mad about what?"

Evelyn had long, flame-red hair that she was shaking back from her forehead.

All of the anxiety that had been coursing through Cory's veins sprang to her features, her voice becoming something like a shouting whisper.

"I think I met somebody."

Evelyn's eyes grew wide. "You dog. How did you meet her?"

A smile found Cory's lips. "I'm waiting on her table."

"She's here?" Evelyn jumped up and began scanning the restaurant. Cory grabbed her arm and pulled her back to her seat.

"Don't look!" Cory maintained her screaming whisper.

"But I have to. Where is she?" Again she stood.

Again Cory pulled her back to her seat. "You can look at her in a minute." She gave Evelyn's shoulders a quick shake. "What should I do?"

"About what?"

"She wants me to join her for dessert."

"Ooh, baby." Evelyn's eyebrows danced. "What kind of dessert does she have in mind?"

"Stop being a pig," Cory hissed. "I need your help."

Evelyn finally saw the anxiety on Cory's face. "Honey, what's wrong?"

"I told her I'd have dessert with her."

"Yeah. And . . ." Evelyn stared.

"I invited all you guys here tonight. I can't just go sit with her and ignore all of you."

Evelyn frowned briefly. "Hmm. When was the last time you had a date, girl?"

Cory rolled her eyes. "Forever."

14

"Exactly. I think we'll be able to forgive you." Evelyn tapped the table with two fingers, her mind racing. "But I need to have a look before I give you my blessing." She stood up, backing away from Cory's reach. "Which one is she?"

Cory groaned. "She's alone, behind the first pillar by the window. Black hair."

Evelyn nodded, stepping away. "Gotta run to the rest room. Be right back."

Cory groaned again and cradled her head in the crook of her arm.

Within moments, Evelyn was sitting across from her again, her face a careful mask.

"First of all, let me just say that I firmly believe that looks are not everything. In fact, they are not important at all." She leaned forward, taking a deep breath and dropping her voice down to a husky whisper. "But damn, woman. She is a babe."

Cory rolled her eyes.

"What are you thinking? Of course you'll have dessert with her. And if you don't, introduce me and I will."

Cory eyed her friend. "She's pretty, isn't she?"

"Understatement. No wonder you have that yippy-skippy look all over your face. She's hot." She ran her hand through her thick red hair, pulling it off her face. "Not that looks matter, of course," she said primly.

"She's got a really nice accent. English or Australian or something."

"Stop it," Evelyn cringed. "You're making me sweat."

"You are such a pig, Evelyn."

Evelyn shrugged. "You love me in spite of it."

"I love you *because* of it," Cory grinned.

"Enough. Go away. Have fun."

"So you won't be mad at me?"

"God, no." Evelyn shooed her away. "I'll explain it to everyone. Don't worry."

"You're not going to sit over here and stare at us all night, are you?" Cory grimaced at the thought.

"Unfortunately, that damn pillar is in the way of my line of sight." She clucked her tongue. "But I do have a weak bladder, so I may have to go to the rest room a lot." She threw back her head and laughed. "Scoot. I'll talk to you later."

Relieved, Cory gave her friend a quick hug before disappearing into the kitchen to regain her composure. Once there, she took a couple of deep breaths to steady herself before stepping back out onto the floor of the restaurant.

She approached Julia from behind, noting that the table had been cleared of all dishes. Cory tried to keep the nervousness out of her voice as she smiled.

"Sorry to keep you waiting. Is there anything else I can get you?" She braced herself for the letdown. She just knew that this woman was going to pay her bill and walk out of her life.

With one finger, Julia pushed the sleeve of her sweater back from her wrist. She studied her watch intently before smiling sweetly up at Cory. "If I'm not mistaken, your shift is officially over, is it not?"

Cory nodded. "In about five minutes. I just have to finish up."

Julia's smile was slow. "Do you like coffee?"

Cory smiled and nodded.

"Good. Then I'd like two cups of coffee and a slice of the chocolate raspberry cheesecake." She held up two fingers. "And two forks. And the check, please."

Grinning, Cory inclined her head. "Whatever the customer wishes, ma'am." She nearly skipped her way back to the kitchen.

She returned moments later, carefully placing Julia's order on the table and hesitating only briefly.

"May I join you?" she ventured.

"Please do." Julia's smile was soft as she pushed the cheesecake to the center of the table and placed a fork in Cory's hand.

"Cory is an interesting name," she began. "I don't believe I've ever heard it before. Is it short for something?"

Cory grimaced. "Corinne," she said flatly. "But I really hate that name." She poured cream into her coffee cup, watching the liquid turn light brown. "What about you? You haven't told me your name yet." She took a small bite of the cheesecake and watched the other woman.

"My friends call me Jules."

"Jules." She liked the name instantly, thinking it most fitting. "Is it short for Julie?"

Julia chose not to answer directly. "I prefer Jules now, I suppose. I'm so used to it."

"And you're from England?"

"Born and raised, I'm afraid." She lifted her mug of coffee and raised it to her lips with both hands.

"When did you move here?" Cory chided herself

17

when she saw a small frown appear between Julia's eyebrows. She was asking too many questions, she decided, and told herself to slow down.

Julia dropped her eyes, hating the inevitable conversation that would follow.

"I don't live here, actually. I'm here for work."

Cory felt her heart sink a little. She should have known this was too good to be true. Already she could see the heartache ahead.

"What do you do?" She hoped that Julia wouldn't hear the disappointment in her voice.

This was the part that Julia hated. She could justify not quite telling the truth, but telling an out-and-out lie still wasn't easy. She took a deep breath.

"I do work for British Airways." She settled the cup of coffee back onto the tabletop, where she kept both hands loosely draped around it. "I'm forever bouncing back and forth between the States and my home." She tried to justify the lie in her mind, reminding herself that she had, in fact, done different advertising covers for the airline. So maybe it wasn't a complete and total lie.

Cory was relieved. Almost. "So you're here quite often then?"

"Quite," Julia nodded, while inside she began the reprimand. Cory was a sweet woman, and here she was lying to her. Bold faced.

Cory settled back in her chair, growing pensive. Common sense was beginning to rear its head, telling her that she didn't need this kind of involvement. That she knew where this was heading.

Sensing her withdrawal, Julia leaned forward to get her attention. "I'm usually here for several days at a time. In fact, this time I'm here for the weekend. My flight leaves on Monday."

Cory's mind did a quick calculation. Today is Friday. She leaves Monday. Three nights. *This is crazy.*

"Do you have a lover?"

Cory's head snapped back, caught off guard by the question. She stared into Julia's eyes, squinting to better see the color.

"I'm sorry," Julia started. "That was rude."

"Oh no. Don't worry," Cory waved the apology aside. "And no. I don't have a lover." She watched, holding her breath as Julia reached across the table and, with one finger, traced the outline of the knuckles on Cory's left hand.

"What about you?" A rushing sound filled her ears as she watched the single fingertip find its way to her wrist.

"No, Cory." Julia let her eyes flutter up to meet Cory's. She looked deadly serious. "I have no lover."

Cory felt the blood pounding in her chest. *This can't be happening,* she told herself again.

Julia's hand covered hers, and Cory raised her eyes to meet Julia's steady gaze.

"Will you spend the weekend with me?"

This is crazy. She wanted to say the words out loud but couldn't. Julia would probably think she was being silly, that she was young and naive.

When Cory didn't reply, uncertainty came over Julia. How dare she assume that it would be so easy? What made her think that Cory would be so willing to fall into her bed?

I'm too old for this. "I'm sorry." She pulled her hand away and was surprised when Cory retrieved it and wrapped it in her own.

"No, please," Cory stammered. "Don't be sorry. I'm just so surprised. I mean, you're so, so . . ."

"Old?" Julia raised a fine brow.

"No!" Cory continued to search for the right words. "You're gorgeous. You just seem so, I don't know, so sophisticated. I don't think I've ever met anyone like you. You're from England. You could have anyone in this place that you wanted."

"And you're adorable and charming and extremely sexy."

Cory's cheeks grew hot again.

"Especially when you blush like that." Julia's smile was lopsided as she teased the younger woman.

"Cory!"

Cory tore her eyes from Julia's in time to see Evelyn approaching their table. She was grinning naughtily when she reached them.

"I thought I saw you over here. How are you?" She continued to smile, trying not to let her eyes wander to the woman sitting across the table from her friend.

Cory groaned inwardly. "Hi, Evelyn. I'm fine."

Evelyn couldn't resist even a moment longer. She turned her attention to Julia, her eyes raking over the other woman's features in one swoop.

"I don't believe we've met." She smiled and offered her hand.

Julia slid a quick glance at Cory before taking the hand in hers.

"This is Jules, Evelyn."

"A pleasure." Julia inclined her head, the smile on her face well practiced.

Evelyn continued to stare far longer than was

polite, until Cory couldn't take it anymore and groaned aloud.

"You'll have to forgive my friend, Jules." She swallowed her pride and continued to explain. "We were actually supposed to meet here for drinks tonight, and she very kindly let me off the hook when you asked me to join you."

Realization dawned, and Julia smiled good-naturedly. "She begged off on you, eh?"

"She did," Evelyn grinned. "But I can see why, and I've forgiven her already."

Julia laughed, accepting the backhanded compliment gracefully. "Then I suppose I should thank you for sharing her with me tonight."

Evelyn shrugged, and Cory decided to needle her a bit.

"I'm afraid that Evelyn is just here to ogle you," she told Julia.

"Ogle me?" The crease appeared between Julia's brows.

Evelyn's laugh was throaty. "She means I just wanted to check you out."

Julia joined her laughter, only slightly embarrassed. "And do I check out okay?"

Evelyn flashed her a thumbs-up.

"Evelyn . . ." Cory gritted out her name between clenched teeth.

Evelyn responded by raising both hands and taking a step back. "Okay, okay. I apologize for intruding."

"No intrusion at all." Julia's hand touched Evelyn's breifly. "I was just trying to convince your friend that she should spend the weekend with me."

Cory blushed clear to the roots of her hair while

Evelyn's eyes grew wide. Her eyes moved from Julia to Cory while she shook her head.

"I can't believe that she'd need much convincing. But if she turns you down, you can find me in the bar, honey." She threw Julia a lascivious look while Cory groaned again.

"Have a nice weekend, Cory." Evelyn winked quickly and turned back to Julia. "Nice meeting you, Jules."

Julia returned the sentiment, and Evelyn was smiling as she retreated to the bar.

"I am so sorry," Cory began.

Julia waved off the apology. "She's quite cheeky, isn't she?"

"You noticed?"

"I'll bet she's great fun."

"She is," Cory agreed. "And you were rather cheeky yourself, I might add."

Julia feigned remorse. "I *was* rather naughty again, wasn't I?"

"You were definitely keeping up with her. Are you naughty all the time?" Cory was finally beginning to relax.

"Only when I'm relaxing and enjoying myself." Julia lifted her coffee mug to her lips. "And right now I'm enjoying myself very much." She took a sip of the hot liquid and returned the mug to the table. "So what do you think? Do you have plans for the weekend?"

Cory was immensely flattered but uncomfortable. Jules was leaving little doubt about what the weekend included. As often as Cory might have fantasized about a wild weekend of passionate sex with a stranger, she didn't think she was actually capable of doing it.

"Nope. No plans so far."

Julia sensed Cory's uneasiness and felt a familiar challenge. Putting on what she was sure was her most dazzling smile, she leaned forward.

"I promise I don't bite." She lowered her voice seductively. "Unless you're into that sort of thing, of course. Then I might perhaps be persuaded."

Cory nearly choked on her coffee. She tried to smile, unsure of herself, knowing she was already in way over her head.

Chapter 3

After some maneuvering and manipulation on Julia's part, they left the restaurant and were soon in Cory's car, heading toward her apartment.

Cory had seemed reluctant to go back to her place. But Julia had been persistent, saying how tired she was of the stark walls in hotel rooms. Cory thought the idea of a hotel with room service would be a treat, but Julia would have no part of it.

The truth was that Julia had learned long ago never to bring a woman back to her own room. If the weekend soured, it was always easier to leave someone than it was to get someone to leave.

Cory lived on the ground level of a two-family home in Watertown, a suburb just outside of Boston off the Massachusetts turnpike. In less than fifteen minutes, she was nervously placing a key in the lock of her front door.

Julia followed her inside, giving the apartment only a cursory glance as she focused all of her energy on finding, and getting Cory to, the bedroom.

"Can I get you something to drink?" Cory asked nervously as she flipped a light switch.

Julia shook her head and reached out to gather Cory in her arms.

Cory wasn't sure what it was that she was feeling as Julia began to drop slow, lingering kisses along her neck. She wanted to feel arousal. Passion. But instead she felt rising panic.

After several moments, Julia raised her head long enough to whisper, "Where's the bedroom?"

Numbly, Cory turned and led the way down the short hallway to her bedroom. She reached over to turn on the bedside lamp, and tried to hide her shock when she saw that Julia was already pulling the camel sweater over her head.

Cory kept her eyes trained on Julia's, unable to let her eyes wander over the other woman's body. Julia's expression seemed matter-of-fact as she reached over and gave a quick tug on the waist of Cory's jeans.

"I don't think you'll be needing those, do you?" she asked.

Tongue-tied, Cory sat down on the bed and began stripping off her shoes, socks, and jeans. Desperately wanting something to cover her seminakedness, she crawled beneath the covers.

When Julia joined her, Cory's anxiety mounted. The other woman was completely naked.

Julia smiled as she toyed with the collar of Cory's shirt.

"You're a rather shy one, aren't you?" Julia was keenly aware of the awkwardness of the situation. It didn't usually go like this. Women usually fell hungrily into her arms. Perhaps she'd misjudged Cory. Maybe it had been a mistake to try to cajole her the way she had.

Dammit. She felt like she was practically forcing herself on the woman.

"This is moving too fast for you, isn't it?" Julia looked into Cory's wide eyes and felt an odd stirring in her chest.

Cory turned her face into the crook of Julia's arm. "I'm sorry." She felt foolish. How could she have let this happen? It's not as though she hadn't known what to expect. Jules had made her intentions clear from the beginning.

Julia frowned and reached up to tuck a curl behind Cory's ear. "Stop apologizing," she whispered. "There's no need."

Her words made Cory feel worse. "I'm being silly. You must think I'm some kind of child or something."

"I think nothing of the sort." Julia's smile was soft. "I'm sorry that I pushed so hard."

Cory kept her eyes hidden. "I've never done this before," she admitted.

"What?" Julia was horrified. *Good god, I nearly seduced a virgin.* Unconsciously, she pushed away from Cory.

"No, no." Cory's eyes flew open and she reached up to pull Julia closer. Then she laughed. "I don't mean I've never done *it*. I mean I've never slept with anyone that I only just met."

Julia chuckled, her laughter throaty. "You had me scared for a moment there." Then she grew serious as she contemplated the woman in her arms. How many times had she herself slept with a woman after only knowing her for a few hours? She couldn't even begin to count the number. Then her mind moved on as she recalled how deliberately she had set out to find a woman tonight. How she had taken one look at Cory and then set out to seduce her, to reel her in. In a brief moment she hated herself for the deceptions, for the old and tired game.

Then she pushed aside her thoughts as quickly as she had let them seep in. It wasn't like her to feel remorse. She leaned over and very carefully placed a closed-mouth kiss on Cory's lips.

"It's all right, you know. Do you want me to leave?"

"No." Cory was adamant. That was the last thing she wanted. "Please don't. Can we just talk for a while?"

"Of course we can." Julia felt oddly relieved and strangely protective.

"Can we hold each other?"

"Of course." Julia smiled. Then she lay down on her back and pulled Cory with her, until Cory's face was buried in her neck.

Cory placed a hand at the base of Julia's throat, content to feel the pulse beneath her fingertips. "You're not too disappointed?"

Julia stared up through the darkness toward the

ceiling, contemplating the question, and surprising herself when she answered honestly. "No, sweetie, I'm not," she sighed and dropped a quick kiss on Cory's brow. "But it is rather nice to hold you."

Chapter 4

Morning came not only early, but awkwardly. Cory woke with a start, immediately aware of the slow and steady breathing of the woman beside her. Her first response was a pounding heart, followed quickly by a silent groan.

I can't believe what an idiot I was last night, she admonished herself. *I have this gorgeous woman in my bed, in my arms, and I chicken out.* She turned her head just enough to sneak a peek at the woman beside her. She was lying on her side, her face toward Cory, both hands hidden under the pillow that cradled her head. Cory closed her eyes and moaned again. *She's even gorgeous first thing in the morning. With her eyes closed.*

Cory's mind moved forward as she contemplated what to do now that she was wide awake. She should do something. Maybe reach over and make a move on her. Stroke her cheek or slide an arm around her waist. Anything. She agonized for some time, certain that Julia thought she was infantile, convinced that Julia would leave as soon as she awoke. *And I'll never see her again. Idiot!*

But she was paralyzed. Too paralyzed to reach out to Julia, and too anxious to lie there and listen to the quiet breathing.

Carefully, she lifted the blankets and slipped her feet to the floor. Then she crept her way to the door and pulled it closed behind her.

Julia opened one eye and listened to the door closing behind her. She stared at the empty pillow beside her before slipping one hand out from under her head and sliding it along the sheet until it lay, palm down, on the heat that remained from Cory's body.

Cory was more hopeful once she'd taken a shower. Wrapped in a thick terry robe, she padded her way out to the small galley kitchen and made coffee. While her mind drifted back to the bedroom, she suddenly remembered that her article would be in the newspaper that morning. Without another thought, she rushed down the hallway to the front door, unbolted the lock, and left the door wide open as she ran down the short stairway and flung open the heavy door that led outside.

Two folded newspapers lay carelessly on the stoop, and she bent to retrieve one copy, mindless of the bathrobe that threatened to come undone.

She waited until she was back in her apartment and sitting at the kitchen table before she carefully turned back the front page.

There it was. Just as Edgar had promised. Just above the fold. "A Dog gone Shame," by Cory Hayes. Her first byline. "Wow," she said aloud, a wide grin springing to her lips. "I could have come up with a better headline. But I guess it will do." She laughed. She read her name over and over before scanning the article, checking to see what had been edited out. But nothing had. Her words were intact, just as she'd written them.

She became aware of a sudden silence in the apartment and realized that the shower had just been turned off. Then she remembered Julia, and decided that she couldn't be in too big of a hurry to leave if she'd taken the time to shower. *Maybe last night wasn't such a complete disaster after all.*

She pushed herself back from the table and had begun pouring coffee when she heard the sound of someone clearing her throat. Glancing toward the hallway, she caught sight of Julia looking almost embarrassed and clutching a towel to her chest. She was breathtaking.

"Hi," Cory grinned.

"Good morning." She squinted at the younger woman sheepishly. "I don't suppose you have something clean that I might be able to borrow? I hate to get back into those clothes I was wearing last night." Her accent was thicker than Cory remembered.

"Of course," Cory quickly brushed past her as she headed back to the bedroom. "Would you like jeans? Maybe sweats? It's a little chilly out for shorts."

She was riffling through a drawer when Julia joined her. "How about these?" She held up a pair of jeans. "They're probably too big for you."

Julia smiled. "Not too big. Just comfortable." She reached out one hand to take the jeans. "Don't want them too tight with no undies on." She laughed at the look on Cory's face. "Don't worry. I don't mind going without."

Cory turned her back the moment she saw that Julia was about to drop the towel. She pulled open another drawer and rummaged through it until she found a soft, red pullover sweater. Thinking it would look good with Julia's dark hair, she held it out without turning around.

"This okay?"

Julia took the sweater from Cory's outstretched hand and shook it out. "Perfect." She pulled it over her head and shook her damp curls before reaching for the zipper of her jeans.

Sensing it was safe, Cory slowly turned and let her eyes take in the other woman. She still couldn't believe it. What would a woman like this want with a woman like her?

"Everything fits." Julia smiled and pushed the sleeves of the sweater to her forearms.

"Well, kind of." Cory was staring at Julia's ankles. "I guess you're a bit taller than me."

Julia glanced down and laughed at the sight of milky white legs exposed for some three inches above her ankles. "Not exactly fashionable, am I?" She glanced up and caught the frown on Cory's lips. "You don't think this will start a new trend?"

Cory caught the smile in her eyes and grinned, shaking her head.

"Oh," Julia feigned offense. "Embarrassed to be seen with me, are you?"

Cory nodded. "Fashion police are all over Boston, you know."

Julia loved the carefree feeling that seemed to hover over her. She couldn't recall the last time she'd felt so silly. "It's my weekend off. I refuse to be a slave to fashion."

Cory tilted her head and clucked her tongue. "Well, you certainly don't have to worry about that."

"Oh," Julia's hands went to her hips. "You are a cheeky thing, aren't you."

Cory grinned. "I've been accused of that before, I'm afraid."

"Hmm." Julia reached out both hands and grasped the lapels of the bathrobe that Cory wore. She leaned in closely until their bodies were nearly touching. "Not the shy little innocent that you were last night, eh?"

As soon as she said the words, she regretted it. Cory's eyes clouded over and her smile faltered. "I'm sorry —"

"Oh damn. I did it again." Julia held her at arm's length and stared directly into her eyes. "I was joking. Please don't take that the wrong way. Last night was quite lovely."

Cory returned the steady gaze, courage returning. "I thought you'd be up and out of here as soon as possible this morning."

Julia's smile was slow. "You won't be rid of me that easily. Not before coffee, anyway."

Cory smiled, beginning to appreciate Julia's sense of humor. "I thought you English types only drank tea."

"It's true. Most do. But I learned long ago that when I travel there's no point. The rest of the world drinks coffee."

Cory studied her face, for the first time noticing the faint freckles across the bridge of her nose. Then she lifted both hands and awkwardly placed them on Julia's hips.

"So you don't hate me?" She was an insecure little girl once again.

Julia raised a finger to stroke her cheek. She acted as if she was contemplating the question seriously. Finally, she raised one brow and tipped her head to one side. "You, I like. It's your jeans that I hate." She leaned over and dropped a quick peck on the end of Cory's nose before turning on her heel. "I'll pour some coffee while you get dressed. Don't be too long."

Cory took her time getting dressed and drying her hair. Glad she'd done her laundry just two days before, she pulled her favorite pair of blue jeans from where they still lay in the laundry basket and slipped them on. Then she pulled her favorite V-neck sweater on over a T-shirt. After leaning over and shaking out her thick brown hair, she took a deep breath, nodded at her reflection in the mirror, and walked down the hall to join Julia.

Julia was bent over the newspaper, a cup of coffee in one hand. Cory approached her from behind and was unable to resist the temptation to put her hands on the lean shoulders. She smiled when Julia

34

rewarded her by raising her hands and pulling Cory's arms around her neck. Cory squatted down, folding her arms across Julia's chest. She peered over Julia's shoulder, scanning the international news page that the other woman seemed to be studying.

Julia sighed and leaned her head back, her cheek pressing against Cory's. "This feels quite nice," she said, causing Cory's heart to flutter. "You have a lovely flat. I didn't really get a chance to see it last night."

It took Cory a moment or two before she realized that Julia was referring to her apartment.

"Oh. The apartment." She glanced around. "It's small. I'd really like to get something bigger someday." She wrinkled her nose. "When I can afford it."

Julia seemed to contemplate the younger woman's words before releasing her arms. Reluctantly, Cory stood up and moved to the chair beside her. A steaming mug of coffee was sitting on the table directly in front of her. She took a sip while Julia turned another page of the newspaper.

Then Julia raised her eyes to Cory's. "I'm embarrassed to ask, but did you ever tell me your last name?"

Cory shook her head. "I don't think so. It's Hayes."

Julia quickly flipped back several pages in the newspaper until Cory's article was displayed. She tapped the article with one finger and narrowed her gaze at Cory.

"Are you this Cory Hayes?"

Cory colored, pride and embarrassment competing. She dipped her head and nodded.

"You're a writer? And a waitress as well?"

Cory shook her head and explained. "I work at the paper. I just fill in at the café whenever they need someone."

Julia smiled. "So last night really *was* my lucky night then, wasn't it?"

Cory took a deep breath. "No. I think it was mine."

"It was *our* lucky night." Julia grinned. "So you're a writer." She stared hard as Cory tried to hold her gaze. "Are you some sort of celebrity, then? What else are you hiding from me?"

Cory laughed. "No. This is my first real story. My first byline, anyway."

"Your first?"

Cory nodded and reluctantly told Julia her story. When she finished, Julia was absolutely beaming.

"How exciting for you. Congratulations." She reached over and covered Cory's hand with her own. "You should be celebrating today. Do you have any plans?"

Cory shook her head.

"Then we must make some. You must let me take you to dinner tonight." Julia was clearly excited.

Cory watched Julia's excitement with growing enthusiasm. Why had she been so worried that Julia would leave that morning? She glanced at the clock on the kitchen wall. "Okay. But what would you like to do for the next ten hours?"

Julia's mind went instantly to the bedroom, but she held her tongue. Instead, she raised a brow and grinned. "Lucky for you that I promised myself that I would steer clear of all sexual innuendo today."

Well, Cory thought, *I wouldn't exactly consider that lucky . . .*

"So since I'm going to do my best to behave, you should probably get me out of here quickly. Perhaps a tour of Boston?"

Cory groaned. "Not the Freedom Trail."

"No, no. Not the tourist stuff. Your Boston," her smile was charming. "Show me what you like to do."

Cory felt her heart constricting. She couldn't believe that Jules would want simply to wander around the city with her. She felt at a loss.

"I know!" Julia grew more animated. "Take me to the animal shelter. I'd love to see some of the pups that you rescued."

Cory thought for only a moment. "We could do that. Then maybe go for a walk along the Charles River. Then how about the North End for dinner?"

"Perfect. Shall I get my jacket?"

"Whoa. Not yet. I need to eat some breakfast first. What about you? I've got toast, cereal."

Julia grimaced. "I can't eat a thing before noon. But you go ahead." She leaned over and pressed a kiss to Cory's cheek. "Go on. Scoot. I'm going to enjoy your article again while I observe your prowess in the kitchen." She winked playfully, and Cory chuckled as she pushed back her chair.

Chapter 5

Julia tried not to let the thought of wearing jeans three inches too short bother her sense of fashion. But she failed. The first thing the couple did once they left Cory's apartment was turn the car around and head back into downtown Boston.

Once in her hotel room, Julia did a quick once-over to make sure that no telltale signs of her deception lay about. Satisfied that the maid had picked up nicely, she took her time swapping Cory's jeans for a pair of her own.

She eyed the closet of clothing briefly before turning back to Cory.

"Would it be presumptuous of me to pack a few things to bring with me? I'd rather not have to stop back here later if we don't have to." She couldn't quite believe it, but she actually felt shy.

Cory smiled, realizing that she was growing more comfortable with Julia. "Sure. Bring something for dinner. Nothing too fancy."

Julia nodded and slipped a linen suit from where it hung in the closet and tossed it onto the bed. Then she grabbed an overnight bag and placed a matching pair of shoes inside. Finally, she opened a drawer and tossed some undergarments into the bag as well.

"Should you bring something for tomorrow?" Confidence growing, Cory feigned shyness. "That is, of course, if you don't have any plans."

The color of Julia's eyes seemed to grow darker as she smiled. "I told you. You have me for the entire weekend if you like."

Cory did a quick calculation. The weekend was already slipping away. "I like," she said simply, and reached out to take Julia in her arms.

Their kiss was slow and tentative as they stared into each other's wide-open eyes. Julia felt instant heat, and she carefully slipped her hands to Cory's face, pushing her mouth away.

"If we get started," she began huskily, "I won't stop. I promise you that. And we have places to see and puppies to visit." *What was I thinking?*

Cory sighed, damning herself for pushing Julia away the night before. *What had I been thinking?*

"I suppose you're right," she managed, even

though at that moment she didn't care if she ever saw the world beyond those four walls again.

Then Julia caught her off guard, kissing her once, hard, before going back to the task of packing. Cory felt as though the wind had been knocked right out of her.

The animal shelter was located on the town line between Brighton and Cory's home in Watertown. The two suburbs were actually closer to Cambridge than to the city of Boston.

Cory was greeted by the staff with a hero's welcome.

"You wouldn't believe it. We rescued nearly thirty animals, and there are only six or so left. Nearly a dozen went just this morning." Deb Peters, the director of the shelter and an old friend of Cory's, was beaming. "Your article was just fabulous. I can't believe the response we've had."

"I'm so glad." Cory was jubilant. She introduced Julia before quickly rushing on. "We thought we would stop by and visit the pups. But I guess there aren't many left?"

"Not many. You'd be surprised at how well most of them seem to be adapting after we cleaned them up and gave them some affection."

"Then they're adjusting all right? Not too timid or shy?" Julia pushed her hands into the pockets of her jacket.

Deb blinked, suddenly aware of Julia's presence. She glanced quickly from one woman to the other, trying to assess their relationship. "Nice accent," she began, then quickly moved on. "Most of the dogs seem to have adjusted okay. Some of the ones still here are shy. Two almost cower when you try to love on them."

Julia frowned. "Do you have any idea what kind of punishment the man who did this will receive?"

Deb shook her head. "No more than we knew before. But the D.A. has been in twice to talk to me. He seems to think that they'll go for full prosecution."

Two other staff members kept running by, going back and forth between the front office and the barking that could be heard from behind the door to the kennels. Loud, deep barks were mixed with quieter whining and yipping. The bell above the front door jingled, and a small family shuffled inside. Another staff member came out of the office to greet them.

"I can't believe how crazy it is around here," Deb was saying. "It's usually so quiet."

Another dog added his voice to the others.

"Well," Deb rolled her eyes. "Not *that* quiet."

Cory, who had been quietly observing the conversation between Julia and Deb, stepped forward. "Would it be okay if we went back and visited them?"

"By all means," Deb said.

"I think we ought to," Julia smiled, "before there aren't any more left to visit." She put her hand on Cory's elbow, urging her toward the kennels.

Once on the other side of the door, they noted that another couple was already there, poking fingers into cages and speaking in high, coddling tones.

Cory and Julia visited each cage one by one. Cory felt her heart tighten as she watched Julia approach each animal.

Julia spoke softly to each one, cooing and chatting until she got a response. The tail of a German shepherd thwacked against the side of his cage the moment Julia gave him her attention. A cocker spaniel puppy pressed herself against the back of her cage, and Julia's heart went out to her.

"Poor thing," she said. "I hope you can find an especially nice home. With parents that will give you more love than a puppy could possible stand."

The puppy lifted her eyes to Julia's. "This breaks my heart," Julia said. It was obvious by the look in her eyes and the sound of her voice that it did just that. Cory watched the compassion on the other woman's features and felt herself go warm. *I could really, really like this woman.*

Deb was opening up one of the cages farther down the hallway. She was squatting down, urging the dog inside to come out and meet the couple who was there before them.

"Come on, sweetie."

Cory and Julia watched as first a nose and then a tentative paw reached outside of the cage. Slowly, the golden retriever found her way into the hallway. She seemed to eye the couple warily as she stood her ground beside Deb.

"She's very gentle," Deb was saying in a soothing voice as she stroked the dog's chest. "She's only about a year and a half old."

The couple bent down, holding out their hands for the dog's inspection. Cory and Julia began inching closer, watching the interaction with interest.

The dog was sniffing the woman's hand. Apparently satisfied, the dog turned her attention to the man. "We were looking for an older dog, hopefully one that's already housebroken."

The man beside her was reaching under the dog's chin, stroking it softly.

"Unfortunately, because of the way these dogs were raised, I can't say whether or not they're trained." Deb frowned. "But I wouldn't bet on it. She's spent most of her life cooped up in a cage no bigger than this one."

As Deb continued to talk, Cory and Julia watched as the couple inched closer to the dog, rubbing her coat and searching her eyes.

"She should be spayed. She had a litter about three or four months ago."

"She's very sweet." The woman moved to stroke the dog's chest.

"Are they difficult to train at this age?" The man asked.

"She shouldn't be too difficult, although all of these dogs are going to need a little extra attention."

The woman sighed and leaned back on her heels, dropping her hands to knees. At first the dog seemed indifferent, but then she lifted a paw and reached out, tapping the hand that had just left her.

Cory and Julia watched the transformation on the women's features. "Oh, Bill. Did you see that?" She placed both hands on the dog's coat and rubbed gently.

Bill was smiling. "Is she the one, Shirley?"

"I think she is," Shirley replied quickly.

Deb stood up. "Why don't I get one of the guys to take all of you out back in the yard. Maybe you can play for a while and get to know each other a bit."

"That would be great," Bill nodded.

Deb left for a moment and returned with another

staff member, whom the couple followed down the hall to the door outside. The tail that belonged to the golden retriever was swishing back and forth as she followed her new parents.

"I don't think I can take it." Julia raised a hand to cover her chest. Cory thought she saw glistening in her eyes. "It's all so happy and sad at the same time."

"It's hard sometimes," Deb replied. "Especially when we can't find homes for them. We've been really lucky with this bunch. We're very fortunate." She turned to Cory. "Thanks again. You just don't know what it means to all of us."

Cory didn't know how to respond. To her it had been an easy decision to write the story and to try to do something to rescue the dogs. The hard part had been getting the story published.

"You said she just had a litter," Cory began, choosing to sidestep the woman's thanks. "Were the puppies with her? Were you able to find homes for them?"

Deb nodded. "She had four pups that we know of. They are so adorable that we didn't have much trouble finding people to adopt three of them."

"What about the fourth?" Julia asked, fearing the worst.

Deb grimaced. "I'm afraid she's going to be a bit more difficult to place."

"Is she sick? Was she beaten?" Julia's voice was grave.

Not quite knowing how to answer, Deb motioned for them to follow her. She moved about six yards away and stopped in front of a cage that was eye level. Peering inside, she waited for the others to join her.

The eyes that peered up at Cory were perhaps the saddest she'd ever seen. The puppy was lying flat on her stomach, her face just inches from the front of the cage. She didn't lift her head, but her eyes moved back and forth between Cory and Julia.

"She's beautiful," Cory murmured. "What's —"

"Her legs," Julia's voice caught in her throat. "What's wrong with her legs?"

Cory's eyes roamed over the puppy's frame, first looking at her front paws, then traveling back to her hind legs, which were completely wrapped in casts from the toes all the way to the hips. The puppy's eyes questioned the onlookers.

Deb opened the front door so that Cory and Julia could get closer without the metal wires in their way.

"She had what's called a luxating patella in both hind legs. That means that her kneecaps won't stay in place without surgical intervention." Deb explained. "It's a birth defect. It often happens to smaller breeds, but it's kind of rare in larger dogs like golden retrievers."

"What exactly is wrong with her?" Julia slowly lifted one hand, palm up, and moved it carefully toward the puppy's nose.

"One of the veterinarians operated on her on Monday to repair her knees. He had to break the bone just below the knee, move it slightly, and then reattach the bone with pins. I know it sounds awful, but it's usually a pretty successful surgery, so we're hopeful."

The small blond face seemed at first uninterested, then lifted only enough to press a cold nose to Julia's outstretched fingers.

"Do you think she'll be okay?" Cory waited a moment before following Julia's lead.

"Like I said, we're hopeful. But it was bad enough that the surgeon was pretty sure that she had never walked before. When we found her she couldn't even stand up for more than a moment or two."

Julia's eyes met Cory's. "This woman is breaking my heart again," she groaned. Then she turned back to Deb. "Do you think you'll be able to find a home for her?"

Now Deb frowned. "It's going to be difficult," she admitted. "She's a very expensive puppy already. The surgery put her price tag at over a thousand dollars."

Cory's whistle was low. Her heart began the strangest hurt. She didn't want to think about what would happen to this puppy if nobody adopted her.

Julia seemed unfazed as she reached in a bit farther and began gently stroking the little girl's ears.

"Hi, sweetie," she cooed. "You're a very pretty girl, do you know that?" She continued to talk to the pup for some time, until she had Cory convinced that the dog was understanding every word.

"May I hold her?" Julia asked Deb.

"You can. But I'm warning you, these puppies are awfully tough to put back once you have one of them in your arms."

Cory felt her heart sink as she watched Deb reach inside the cage and gently lift the puppy. "Watch the legs," Deb said quietly as she placed the pup in Julia's waiting arms.

It seemed to Cory that the puppy didn't quite

know what to think or what to do with herself. She lay unmoving in Julia's arms, her face pointing directly at Cory. Wide brown eyes stared at Cory with helplessness.

"How long before she should be able to try standing and walking?" Julia continued to ask questions.

"We've already started working with her on standing up. I don't expect that she'll really be able to do it on ber own until the casts come off. But we're trying to get her used to it. She'll have to go slow, though. Remember that if she's never really walked before, her legs must be very weak."

The crease between Julia's brows deepened as she lovingly stroked the puppy's back. "I wish I could take her." Her voice was soft and low. Emotions flooded over her. She was wishing not for the first time that her life was more settled. More simple.

Cory lifted a hand to scratch behind the pup's ears. The brown eyes were locked on hers, and Cory couldn't look away even if she wanted to.

Julia turned back to Deb. "Do you think she would be easier to place if her price tag weren't so high?"

Deb wasn't quite sure how to take this question. "Well, probably. But —"

"Then I'd like to make a donation on her behalf, if that's allowed."

Cory heard but couldn't believe it. She blinked and moved her gaze to stare at Julia's serious expression.

"That would be incredible." Deb was clearly taken aback. "That's so generous of you. Of course we'd accept."

"Good. Consider it done, then." Julia turned her attention back to the puppy while Cory met Deb's eyes.

Is she for real? Deb's eyes seemed to ask, and Cory had no response other than a slight shrug of her shoulders. Cory studied Julia's face, wondering about this gorgeous woman with an obviously generous spirit. *And a pocketbook to match, apparently.* Cory wanted to know her. Everything about her. Every single detail.

Julia was sighing. "I have to put you back, sweetpea," she was telling the puppy. Then she turned back to Deb. "Why don't we put her back and go take care of her bill?"

Cory watched Deb reach for the dog before she finally spoke up. "Can I hold her? Just for a few minutes while you take care of everything?" She held out both hands toward the puppy in Julia's hands.

Julia eased the puppy into Cory's outstretched hands, their eyes meeting briefly over the puppy's head. Then Julia gave the dog a small pat before reaching into her pocket and pulling out a tiny wallet.

"Shall we?" She waited for Deb to lead the way, then put a hand briefly to Cory's cheek before following.

Alone now with the little golden retriever, Cory tried to carefully shift her around until the puppy's backside rested in one palm and both front paws were planted firmly on Cory's chest.

"Looks like you got yourself a benefactor," she whispered as she smiled down at the brown eyes. "You have such sad eyes," she said to the eyes that wouldn't leave hers. As she stared down into those eyes, she caught a whiff of puppy breath and had to smile.

She patted the little girl's head and felt the warm breath on her chest where the pup's chin lay. She knew she should put her back in the cage, but she couldn't. Her heart felt heavy.

She dropped her face down until their noses nearly touched, and felt a giggle rise as she felt the warm breath on her face. Her heart was swelling; she could feel it.

Then the little black lips parted and a pink tongue appeared and covered Cory's chin with little wet kisses. Her heart opened and burst in that moment.

By the time Julia reappeared, Cory's mind was made up.

"I want to adopt her."

Julia didn't look a bit surprised. "I was hoping you would."

Deb tried briefly to change her mind. "She's going to be a lot of work. She needs lots of attention and love."

"I have plenty to give her. I promise."

"She's going to be big when she grows up. She'll need a lot of room to run."

"I'm moving soon." She turned to Julia. "Didn't I just tell you that this morning?"

Julia raised a brow. "Indeed. I believe you did. But please don't tell me that we're going to go house shopping today." She laughed.

"Naw," Cory replied. "It can wait until tomorrow."

Julia looked horrified for a brief moment. Then she grinned and began picking out items to purchase — dog food and dog bowls and a crate for training. She paid for the whole lot and then packed up the car, whistling the entire time. Vet appointments were made and papers were passed. And all the while, Cory wouldn't put the puppy down for an instant.

The entire staff came out to see them off. Cory

promised to bring the golden back for a visit soon, and then she debated with Julia for several moments before common sense took over.

"You drive," she told Julia. "The keys are in my pocket."

"I'd love to, sweetie, but I'm not licensed to drive in the States."

Cory did not want to relinquish her new puppy, even for the ride home.

"It's just a few miles. You won't get caught."

Julia was tolerant, smiling easily. "I drive on the left side of the road. I don't think that would go over very big here, do you?"

Cory stared hard, pouting. Reluctantly, she gave in. "All right. I'll drive. But be careful with her, okay?"

Julia's grin just got wider as she got into the car on the passenger side and let Cory carefully place the puppy in her lap.

Chapter 6

"Are you always so impulsive?" Julia's voice was near a whisper.

"You mean the puppy?" Cory shook her head. "No. Never. My friends give me a hard time because I never do anything on the spur of the moment. If I haven't planned it, mapped it out, and beat it to death for weeks, then I usually won't do it."

Julia smiled softly. "I rather thought you might be behaving out of character. I hope I wasn't a bad influence on you."

If she hadn't fallen in love with Julia's melodic

voice before, Cory was certainly beginning to now. She shook her head and laughed. "I don't think so." She thought hard for a moment, unable to decide whether she would have taken the pup if Julia hadn't been there. But then she glanced quickly at the puppy and knew that she would have.

"I think that's why I feel so certain about her. I never react that way about anything."

"Heart of stone?"

"No, I'm a mushball. I just mean that I never make snap decisions. With her, there was no decision to be made. I just knew it was right."

They were sitting on the small braided rug on the living room floor. Julia sat cross-legged, while Cory leaned against the sofa. Her new pet was curled up beside her on the floor, sleeping soundly.

They'd been back at the apartment for several hours. During the entire time they'd sat together in that very spot, trying to get the puppy acquainted with her new surroundings. She had sat quietly in the middle of the rug while her eyes wandered over her new home. Cory and Julia had tried several times to place her on her feet, but she just stared at them with uncertainty before struggling to sit back down. Finally the puppy had lain down, content to have Cory's hand on her neck.

At Deb's suggestion, Cory had called the veterinarian who had performed the surgery on the little golden retriever earlier in the week. The vet had gone over in great detail the surgery he had performed and suggested the best way to help the puppy get back on her feet.

Cory watched the steady breathing as she gently

stroked her puppy's short fur. "The vet said not to push her too hard, and that eventually she'll get used to the idea of standing on her legs. Then when the casts come off we'll work on getting her to stand on her own."

Julia frowned. "I imagine her legs must be awfully weak. Particularly if she's never walked before."

"That reminds me." Cory turned her attention back to Julia. "I want to pay you back every penny that you spent on her. I don't have it all right now, but I can give you a little each month."

"It was really my pleasure. Don't give it a second thought." Julia was instantly uncomfortable.

"Really. I feel bad about this. I don't want you to think that I only took her because you'd already paid the bill."

Julia tried not to be offended, but an edge crept into her voice. "I think no such thing, and you must accept this as a gift. It was my absolute pleasure to do so little, and I don't want to hear any more about it."

Cory stared hard at Julia, seeing this side of her for the first time. Julia's eyes were narrow, her violet eyes dark. Cory struggled with wanting to please her and knowing that she couldn't accept such an expensive gift.

"Jules, that's a lot of money. I barely know you."

Julia almost laughed. During the highlight years of her career, for a single hour of work she'd commanded fifty times what she'd given the shelter. She certainly didn't bring in that kind of money anymore, but she would never have to worry about her future.

"But I didn't give the money to you. I gave it to the shelter." Julia leaned forward and placed her hands on Cory's outstretched legs. "I can afford it easily. I promise. I would gladly have paid double had I known you were going to adopt her."

She hated to admit it, but Cory felt relief. She smiled slowly and nodded. "Okay." She reached out with her unoccupied hand to cover one of Julia's. "Thank you. I'll try to let it go."

"A good idea." Julia pulled herself to her knees and leaned forward until her lips touched Cory's. Then she rocked back on her heels and was satisfied to take in the mental image of Cory sitting before her, eyes wide from the surprise kiss. She glanced briefly at the puppy, noting the way Cory's hand seemed to move along its back unconsciously. Then her eyes met Cory's again and, for the briefest of moments, her heart was full.

"So much for going out to a nice Italian restaurant in the North End. I hope you're not too disappointed." They were sitting side by side on the couch while the puppy lay at Cory's feet.

"What, pizza isn't nice Italian cuisine?" Julia grinned and picked up another slice and raised it to her lips.

"Not this takeout stuff." She took a sip from a can of soda. "I'm sorry about dinner."

Julia eyed Cory momentarily. "Don't be. I wouldn't have it any other way. And why do you keep apologizing to me?"

Cory frowned, feeling contrite. She glanced at the clock, noting that it was nearly eight o'clock, and felt anxiety for Julia's impending departure. So far they'd made no plans beyond the next day, and Cory was growing concerned. She decided to be honest.

"Because I feel like I keep letting you down. First there was last night. Then I messed up the plans we'd made for tonight." She shrugged and took a deep breath. "And I really like being with you, and I'm worried that I've blown this whole weekend and that you can't wait until Monday rolls around so you can make a graceful exit." She took another deep breath, hating herself for feeling so inadequate, and let more words spill. "And we haven't really talked about anything, like when you'll be back in town and when we might see each other again."

Julia narrowed one eye. The distress on Cory's face and in her voice was palpable. This was the inescapable moment that always came. The moment when her weekend fling would raise the inevitable question, *When will I see you again?* Julia waited for the usual hardness to capture her heart, for the boredom and disdain to creep into her mind. She waited, her eyes on Cory. Then she waited some more. But her heart would not grow cold.

"Cory, you haven't messed up anything," she began. "The weekend certainly hasn't turned out the way I'd expected it to either." *Now there's an understatement.* "But I've enjoyed myself. And you."

"You're not too disappointed?" Cory asked.

"No." Julia answered immediately, surprising herself when she realized it was true. "I'm not disappointed at all." She put the unfinished slice of pizza on a paper plate on the coffee table and turned her attention back to Cory.

"In fact," she reached out a hand and placed it along Cory's cheek. "I'm enjoying myself quite a bit,

55

and I'll be sorry when the weekend's over." As sincere as she felt, the moment the words were out she regretted them. *No need to bring up my leaving.* Realizing her mistake, she leaned over and pressed her lips to Cory's, hoping to stifle any more questions.

Chapter 7

Julia opened her eyes abruptly and found herself staring at a vaguely familiar ceiling. As her eyes and mind became oriented, she felt an unfamiliar sinking in her heart. In just twenty-four hours, it would be time to leave. Time to get back to her life.

She closed her eyes and carefully rolled over on her left side, toward the sound of the quiet, even breathing beside her.

Cory was just a few inches away, lying on her back. One arm was tucked beneath the heavy comforter while the other was flung back on the pillow above her head.

Julia let her eyes trace the soft curves of Cory's face. She couldn't quite put her finger on what it was she was feeling, but her instincts told her that it wasn't good. She couldn't explain why or how, but she knew that somehow she'd managed to drop her guard and that she was actually beginning to care about this woman.

She resisted the temptation to trace a finger along Cory's cheek. Instead she quietly studied her features while trying to figure out what made this particular woman different from all those before her.

Maybe it had something to do with the fact that they hadn't actually had sex. Usually, that was *all* she had with the others. Long weekends of endless, steamy passion. But for some reason, mindless sex just somehow seemed wrong with Cory.

First there had been Friday night. *I was really pushing myself on her,* Julia thought, ashamed of her behavior.

Last night when they'd gone to bed, Cory had grown quite amorous. But then the puppy began a quiet whimpering that stole their hearts and dissolved the mood. And Julia had been the one who suggested placing the pup between them. They were both rewarded with soft puppy kisses, the first real sign of affection from their new little friend.

Cory must have put her back in her crate some time during the night, because she was no longer in sight.

Maybe I should get up and leave now. Julia repeated the words several times in her mind while she let her eyes travel over Cory's face for a few moments longer. *My plane doesn't leave until tomorrow morning. If I leave now, I'll just wander around the city depressed.* Decision made, she turned off the voice in her head and lifted a hand to find the softness of Cory's skin beneath her T-shirt. Julia let her fingers tickle the smooth belly until a small grin appeared on Cory's sleepy face. Eyes fluttered open briefly before closing shyly.

"Hi," Cory muttered, then she lifted hands and arms and wrapped herself around Julia, her face buried in the other woman's neck.

"Good morning," Julia whispered. "I couldn't look at you another moment without touching you. I hope you don't mind."

"Mmm, not at all." Cory's lips found the softness of Julia's throat.

Julia felt a physical jolt that she was totally unprepared for. But instead of acting on the passion that had sprung to life, she rolled over to her back, bringing Cory with her. Cory's face was still buried in her neck, but now one leg and one arm curled around Julia's legs and waist as well.

"This feels so nice," Cory said, her voice coarse with the morning.

"It does, doesn't it." Julia closed her eyes and held Cory a bit closer.

"I know I shouldn't say this" — Cory's voice became even quieter — "but I really wish you didn't have to go."

Julia sighed. For a moment, she thought about being honest, about backing up and telling Cory the truth about who she was. Maybe it would be different this time. Maybe she could actually begin a real relationship with Cory. Her career was on its last legs anyway.

"Believe me," Julia said, biting her lip. "I wish I could work out a way to stay." She could feel depression threatening to get the better of her, and she searched for another topic to avoid becoming maudlin.

"Did you put Sophie back in her crate?"

"Sophie?" Cory laughed. They had spent a good hour before falling asleep the night before, trying to come up with the right name for her new pet. "I don't believe we came to any decisions about her new name. And yes, I put her back in her crate in the middle of the night."

Julia smiled. "I still think Sophie is the perfect name for her."

"We'll see," Cory sighed and snuggled even closer to Julia. If she had her way, they wouldn't leave that very spot all day.

They barely did. The bedroom became the center of their day. They left only to take the puppy outside and to make a quick snack. At dinnertime they found themselves together in the kitchen, where Julia peeled vegetables for a salad and Cory rolled out dough to make a loaf of bread.

They ate dinner by candlelight, sitting at the kitchen table while they talked and laughed and held hands.

But before long the night fell, they made their way back to the bedroom. Cory was nervous but never more certain of her feelings, and Julia was filled with dread as she tried to ignore what she knew the morning would bring.

Chapter 8

Cory awoke slowly, listening for any sign that Sophie was awake and stirring. Hearing only the quiet of the apartment, she set about trying to go back to sleep. It was early yet. *Still dark outside.*

She found herself in that place between sleep and wakefulness, her mind spinning fantasies. Somehow she remembered that it was Monday, and that she had to get up and go to work. She groaned in her dreams, wishing she could turn back the clock and make it Saturday again. Then she and Jules could have more time together.

Jules! Her eyes flew open as she bolted upright. The empty pillow beside her sent her mind racing. *She can't be gone already. Not without saying good-bye.*

She threw back the covers, feet hitting the floor in a dead run. There were no lights on in the apartment. Every room was empty. No shower. No coffee. The front door was locked but not bolted.

Cory stared at the locks while the evidence told her what she already knew. Jules was gone. "I can't believe it." She stared at the door for a while longer, her anger mixing with her hurt. "She just snuck out without saying good-bye."

She glanced around the apartment, looking for a note, but found none.

Back in the bedroom, she got down on her knees in front of the crate and opened up the small door. Sophie made a happy, deep-throated sound in greeting as her tail slapped against the side of the cage. Reaching inside, Cory gently scooped her up and held the puppy in her arms, welcoming the soft kisses and the whiskers that tickled her cheek.

"She's gone, Sophie," Cory whispered, trying to stop the tears that flowed freely.

Julia rudely declined the coffee that the flight attendant offered and closed her eyes. *I am an absolute bitch this morning,* she told herself, not caring in the least. She was feeling sorry for herself, and didn't much care about that either. *I am a bitch and a fool and a devious little shit to boot,* she told

62

herself while fighting off the headache that threatened to make her physically ill.

No matter how many times she pushed it away, she kept replaying the morning in her mind. She saw herself waking up again and again. Panic and fear and loathing all swallowing her up and fighting for control.

She had to leave. But it was the last thing she wanted to do. She was convinced that she and Cory could work something out, and she was just moments away from waking Cory and confessing everything. Then she came to her senses.

She knew that if she didn't get up and leave that moment she would wake Cory, spill her guts, and beg for forgiveness.

Quietly, she eased back the covers and put her feet to the floor. She stepped into her jeans and pulled a sweater over her head, carefully bending to pick up her shoes and wallet on her way out of the bedroom. Without looking back, and without thought for the few items of clothing that she'd left behind, she quietly flipped the bolted lock and pulled open the front door.

The crisp air stung her cheeks as she nearly trotted down the street in the direction of the busiest nearby intersection.

She didn't have to wait long for a cab, even at that early hour. By the time she arrived back at the hotel and had taken a shower, the first sign of daylight began to show itself.

It took all of the tricks and training learned over twenty years for her to remain calm and poised as she packed her bags and checked out of the hotel. She steeled her heart and cleared her thoughts as she sat in the cab that carried her to the airport.

She watched as the city came to life, refusing to think about Cory but unable to stop seeing the image of Cory awaking to find her gone. *She must hate me. I shouldn't have left like that. I should have left a note. Anything.*

As she checked her luggage and walked down a long corridor to her departure gate, she refused to glance at the telephones that beckoned her. *I should call her. No, I can't call. What would I say? Gee, sorry I left without saying good-bye. I had a really great time and you must forget about me because I'll never see you again . . .*

Julia realized that she must have groaned aloud when she caught the gentleman across the aisle staring at her.

She turned away from him, chin lifting, and stared out the window at the clouds below. No, she couldn't call Cory. She couldn't send flowers. She couldn't apologize or say thank you. She could only go home. Back to her life. To the only life she'd known for many years.

Chapter 9

Cory was on a mission. Reality had slapped her hard when she was standing outside in her tiny backyard trying to get Sophie to "go potty."

She now had a dog. And a tiny apartment. She had to figure out something, and quick.

She went over and over her plan as she drove into work that morning, careful not to jostle Sophie too much in her crate. She arrived at the office just early enough, and set about putting her plan into action.

No one noticed when she tucked Sophie's crate under her desk and opened the door. Then she carefully reached inside and urged the puppy out and into her arms. She was thankful when no one gave her more than a quizzical look as she gritted her teeth and headed for Edgar's office.

"Morning, boss." She smiled sheepishly from her boss's doorway, watching his reaction carefully as he eyed the puppy in her arms.

"What d'ya got there, kid? And don't tell me it's a present." She took the fact that he hadn't hit the ceiling as a good sign and dared to step inside.

"She's one of the pups that were rescued last week," she told him, inching her way closer to his desk.

His eyes narrowed. "What's wrong with her legs?"

Cory stopped once she reached the side of his desk, adjusting Sophie so that Edgar could see her face.

"Her knees didn't work right, so they had to do surgery. But she should be all right in a few weeks." Sophie was watching Edgar with curiosity, her head lifted as her nose began sniffing the air.

Cory watched the large man carefully, gauging his response. His usual curmudgeon persona seemed to be missing as he reached out a hand for Sophie's inspection.

"Golden's are good dogs. Real gentle and even-tempered." Sophie seemed to approve of him, and Edgar cautiously rubbed her ear. "You trying to find her a home? Or are you keeping her?"

"Well, that depends." Cory took a deep breath and plowed on. "I can't really leave her alone yet. Not until she's had the casts off and is able to get around on her own." She paused, almost losing her nerve. "I know you'll probably think I'm crazy, but I was kind of hoping you'd let me bring her to work with me for a week or two. Just until I know she can get around okay." She could feel her head getting light as she said the words. *I really am crazy this time.*

Edgar snorted as he pulled his hand back and shook his head. "You got balls, kid," he laughed.

Sophie was pawing the air, and Edgar took the hint, rubbing her ear again. "You got a cage or something to keep her in?"

Cory nodded, hope soaring. "It fits right under my desk. She's real quiet."

"Two weeks," Edgar barked. "If she barks or pees on my floor, then she's outta here." He gave Sophie a final pat on the head, dismissing them both.

Cory was grinning. "Edgar. Thank you. She'll be an angel."

"And nobody else better be coming in here asking if they can start bringing their cat to work. You got that?" He was practically growling, his neck bulging over the collar of his white shirt.

"Yes sir," Cory agreed.

"Now get outta here. I got work to do." He bowed his head, but Cory hesitated. She had one more favor to ask.

When she didn't leave, he lifted his head, two bushy eyebrows raised. "You're pushing your luck," he told her.

She smiled nervously. "There's something else."

Edgar heaved a sigh and leaned back in his chair. "What," he demanded.

"I need a raise." She spit the words out quickly. "I need to get a bigger place for me and Sophie, and I can't really afford much right now."

Edgar lifted a hand and snapped. "Spare me the details of your personal life," he barked, then lifted thick fingers to one temple and rubbed. Hard. Cory took a cautious step in retreat. Then without a word, Edgar turned to the computer on his desk and punched several keys. With a couple of clicks of the mouse, he was staring at Cory's employment record.

He drummed his fingers on the desktop for several long moments before pulling out a calculator and punching in a few more numbers. He stared at the results and pushed back his chair.

"I'll make you a staff reporter. That's twenty percent."

Cory's jaw nearly dropped.

Edgar was waving her off again. "You're gonna have to bust your butt and prove yourself. You need a couple of hard news articles. Maybe some investigative pieces. No more fluff pieces."

Cory took two steps backward. "Edgar. That's more than —"

Edgar looked like he was about to split his gut. "You're a good writer." He shrugged, calming down. "Hell, the promotion is probably overdue. Just get back to your desk." He raised a pointed finger and narrowed his eyes. "And don't make me regret this."

"Yes sir. I won't, sir. *You* won't, sir," she stammered. Then Edgar was glowering once again, threatening to get out of his chair.

Cory finally caught the hint and took it. Holding Sophie close to her chest, she turned on one heel and was out of his office before he could utter another word.

Chapter 10

It didn't take long for word to get around the office that Cory was hiding a secret under her desk. Soon everyone was stopping by to greet Sophie, and Cory was beaming like a proud parent. But mindful of Edgar's watchful eye, she made a point of keeping Sophie hidden whenever possible. She didn't want to risk Edgar's wrath for even a moment.

During the regular Monday morning staff meeting, Edgar didn't mention her promotion directly. He sat behind his desk as usual, doling out story assignments to each of the staff writers. As he read off the list of stories to investigate, assigning them as he went, he glanced pointedly at Cory as he rattled off the fourth lead on his list.

"Channel eight got hold of a story about some kind of mail fraud with some elderly folks up in Somerville. I want you to follow up and see what you can find out." He held out a piece of paper with notes scribbled all over it, and Cory took it from his outstretched hand.

Without a beat, Edgar moved on. But Cory sensed the stares from her coworkers, and she felt her ears grow hot. She dared a quick glance around the room and was met with a number of guarded grins and even a couple of thumbs-up.

She was finally getting her chance.

By midafternoon she'd been on the phone for hours, checking out leads and setting up interviews for the morning. At four o'clock, satisfied that she had everything in order and under control for the next day, she flipped on her computer and began sifting through the real estate section of the want ads. She was going to have to get very serious about finding a bigger place as soon as possible.

The phone on her desk began ringing, and she picked it up and put it to her ear.

"Cory Hayes."

"Did you survive the weekend?" Evelyn purred in her ear.

It took a moment for Cory to place the voice, and another moment to follow Evelyn's meaning. *Jules.* So far she'd been able to push thoughts of her away through most of the day.

"Hi, Evelyn."

"So? Did you spend the weekend with her?"

Cory's cheeks grew hot with embarrassment. She glanced around quickly until she was certain that no one was paying any attention to her or to her conversation.

"Yeah," she said simply.

Evelyn responded with a shriek. "My god, she was so hot, Cory! How was it?"

For the first time that day, Cory let her thoughts drift back over the weekend. She sighed as she felt the stirring in her chest.

"Wonderful. She was just wonderful."

"Oh my god. She must have been so good in bed. I envied you all weekend."

"Don't be a pig, Ev," she snipped, then realized that she was actually being defensive about the fact that she and Jules hadn't actually made love.

Evelyn lowered her voice. "Pretty touchy about her already, aren't you? This sounds serious."

Cory sighed, unable to explain, unable to fill the silence.

"Wow, Cory. You didn't fall for her, did you?"

Although Cory hadn't allowed herself to really analyze her feelings, she knew that Evelyn was dead on the mark.

"I think so," she mumbled.

Evelyn's tone grew cautious. "Well, tell me about the weekend, sweetie. What happened?"

Cory didn't know where to start. Her eyes fell to the crate beneath her desk and found a pair of big brown eyes staring up at her.

She blurted out the first words that came to mind. "I got a puppy."

"A puppy?" Evelyn laughed. "Shit, woman. You must have been awfully busy. How did that happen?"

Cory told her about how she and Jules had gone to the shelter on Saturday. Then, with a few nudges from her friend, she told Evelyn some of what she and Jules had shared over the weekend.

"It sounds like you had a wonderful time. That's great Cory." Evelyn paused. "So how did you leave it? When are you going to see her again?"

It dawned on Cory that she had no idea. But feeling foolish, she chose not to tell her friend the complete truth.

"I'm not sure, actually. She had to leave this morning before I got up. Then I was running late and didn't have time to look for a note or anything. I guess I'll figure something out when I get home." She almost believed what she was saying.

"Why don't you just call her?"

Cory froze. Then she swallowed hard and began fidgeting in her chair.

"Um. I don't have her phone number," she admitted.

"What?"

"She probably left it for me at the apartment. Like I said, I'll check when I get home." Growing more and more uncomfortable, Cory just wanted to hang up the phone. She didn't want to think about this now. Not while she was at work.

"But she has your number, right?"

When Cory didn't answer, Evelyn groaned.

"Did you give her your number?" she demanded.

"Well, no." Now she was irritated *and* defensive. "We were going to do all that stuff this morning."

"But you said she left before you got up."

Cory didn't like the protective tone in Evelyn's

72

voice. Or maybe she just didn't like the logical conclusions that she knew Evelyn was drawing. She decided to keep her teeth tightly clamped together.

"I'm coming over," Evelyn was saying. "I'll pick up a pizza and meet you at your place."

"No," Cory practically shouted, her head beginning to pound. She quieted her voice. "No, Ev. I've got to take care of Sophie. And I really think I just need to be alone tonight. A lot's happened the last couple of days. I just need to think."

There was silence on Evelyn's end of the line.

"How about if we get together this weekend?" Cory spent another few minutes attempting to ease Evelyn's fears, and she finally convinced her that she was okay.

By the time they'd finished making arrangements for the weekend, Cory was hanging up the phone and noting that it was nearly four-thirty. She reached a hand down and slid two fingers inside Sophie's cage, giving her a quick scratch on the head. Then she buried her head in the crook of her arm and closed her eyes for a brief moment.

She must have overlooked something that morning, she was certain. She just knew that Jules had left her a note and that she had just missed it somehow. She suddenly wanted to be at home in her apartment so she could search for that note.

One of the good things about working for the paper was that as long as you met your deadlines, employees were pretty much able to come and go as they pleased.

And she pleased.

By the time she reached the parking lot, she had

convinced herself that there was probably not only a note waiting for her but certainly a message from Jules on her answering machine as well.

Whistling, she strapped a seat belt around Sophie's crate before steering her car out of the parking lot and into the evening traffic.

At eight o'clock that night, Cory was sitting on the floor of the living room with Sophie at her side. She had combed the apartment. Once. Twice. Then one more time to make sure, searching everywhere for some kind of note, but she had found none. And no matter how many times she played the messages on her answering machine, she didn't hear Jules' voice even once.

Now she was mindlessly stroking Sophie's back while she stared at all of the evidence she'd gathered that proved Jules had in fact just been there.

The overnight bag that Jules had grabbed from her hotel room on Saturday was still stuffed with a few things. A pair of jeans. Underwear, socks, and a bra. Two pairs of shoes, and a sweater. The linen suit still hung where Jules had placed it in Cory's closet. And the black leather jacket still lay on the overstuffed chair where Jules had carelessly flung it on Saturday.

Cory had turned every pocket inside out and had found nothing even close to personal in nature.

Now she stared at what was left of the weekend in front of her and felt the pressure in her chest begin to tighten. It made no sense. Why would Jules just leave without even taking her clothes? Had she been in that great of a hurry? Maybe there had been an emergency.

She'll call.

No she won't. She doesn't even have my number.

She tried to piece together what she did know about Jules and was amazed at how little she could actually come up with. She had spent over forty-eight hours with the woman and barely knew a damn thing about her.

"Let's see," she began to speak out loud, directing her comments to Sophie. But the sarcasm and recrimination were pointed squarely at herself. "You know that she works for British Airways. You have no idea when she'll be back. You don't know her phone number and don't even have a clue about where she lives. Bright, Cory. Very sharp."

It occurred to her that she should be able to find her. Maybe through the phone listings on the Internet. She was about to jump up and go online when another truth struck her hard. She closed her eyes and lifted both hands to rub them. *I don't even know her fucking last name.*

She wanted to cry. She wanted to let the hot tears escape and roll down her cheeks. She wanted to let loose all of the hurt and frustration. But she was too angry. Angry at herself for being such a fool. For being duped and taken in. For believing that their time together had been something more than just a fling.

Somewhere inside she felt an unreasonable rush of satisfaction. At least they hadn't made love. At least she had that much.

Chapter 11

"Fuck you, Raymond." Julia lifted her chin and stared at her reflection in the mirror while she carefully applied red lipstick.

"Don't play that game with me, Julia. You knew we had a show next week. I can't believe you went and fucking did that to your hair." He stomped a foot for emphasis.

So far she was keeping her cool. Refusing to let him rattle her. She shrugged nonchalantly, continuing to apply the makeup.

"So I'll wear a wig for the show. I've done it before."

"Damn right, you will." He ran a thumb and forefinger over his goatee, then pointed a finger at her reflection. "But I'm warning you now. If it doesn't look right for the spring fashions, I'm pulling you from the show."

Julia rolled her eyes but kept her temper in check. The spring show was an empty threat. It was still nearly five months away. Plenty of time for her hair to grow out and the color to return.

When he didn't get a response from her, he grew more irritated. Standing directly behind her now, he placed both palms on her shoulders and squatted down until their faces were side by side in the mirror.

"I certainly hope she was worth it." He hissed the words against her ear.

She could have slapped him, but she refused to give him the satisfaction. Instead, she smiled sweetly.

"I enjoyed a perfectly lovely weekend, Raymond. Thank you for asking." She blinked twice, punctuating her words.

Raymond scowled. "Just don't get yourself into another mess, my dear. I warned you about your personal life interfering before."

Julia was losing her patience. She raised a single brow as she spoke.

"Isn't it a shame that the same rules don't apply to you and all of the little weekend fucks that you've had over the years."

Now he smiled, grabbing the upper hand.

"Ah, but we both know the difference, sweet Julia." He stretched and brought himself up to full height. "I'm not the product. You are."

She was sick of being referred to as *the product.*

"Yes. But this *product* is thirty-eight years old. And getting awfully tired of being stuck under your thumb."

Raymond's smile was anything but humorous. "Thirty-nine next month, I believe." He crossed his arms in a familiar pose, raising one finger to his lips as he spoke. "Too old for a modeling career, if the truth be told. The designers don't want you any longer, Julia. They only take you on and let you do their shows as a courtesy to me."

Ouch. Julia tried not to cringe, but Raymond could see that he had scored a direct hit.

"Be careful, Julia," he whispered with menace. "I can finish you like that." He snapped his fingers for emphasis.

As she stared at the satisfied smirk on his face, she knew that for the first time in her life she was no longer afraid of what Raymond could do to her. The realization gave her strength and a new freedom.

She tilted her head to one side and flashed him a well-practiced, charming smile. "And would that really be so bad, Raymond? To lose all of this?"

He threw back his head and guffawed. "You would have nothing without this, Julia." He swept out both arms, stepping away from her. "You have no life. No family. No friends." He reached for the door to the dressing room. "You only have me and this career." He smiled while making his exit. "And we both know it, don't we?"

He slammed the door behind him, and Julia continued to stare into the reflection of the mirror for some time.

He was right, of course. Her family was long gone,

scattered across Europe and barely speaking. The only friends she had were the fake friends in the business.

She stared hard into the mirror, watching the muscle in her jaw flex as she tried to calm her anger and frustration. The truth was that if she wanted to pick up the phone that very moment, she wouldn't even know whom to call.

Her mind drifted to Cory, and she tried to calculate the time difference. Cory would still be in bed, she was sure. Julia found herself wondering if Sophie would be tucked in beside her. A smile tugged on her lips. She would be willing to bet money that the two of them were curled up together in Cory's bed.

She held the image in her mind for several moments, enjoying it, trying not to think about how much she wished she were sharing that bed with them both.

Chapter 12

"All right. Let me see if I've got all this right."
Evelyn leaned forward on the couch, toning down her
usual animation.

She began counting off on her fingers. "She told
you her name is Jules. But you don't know if that's
her real name."

Cory shook her head.

"You don't know her last name."

This is hopeless.

"You don't know where she lives. Only that it's somewhere in England."

"Pretty much. Although I don't think she even specifically said England. I just assumed that."

"So she could live in East Africa for all we know."

Cory cringed. "Bingo."

"Well, she must have a lot of money." Evelyn settled back against the cushions and crossed her legs. "She picked up Sophie's tab, and those clothes are not exactly Wal-Mart's house brand."

Cory felt Sophie pawing at her hand, and she smiled, lifting both hands to caress the puppy's face. Both casts had come off Sophie's legs the day before. So far Sophie didn't quite seem to know what to do with herself whenever Cory picked her up and placed her back down on all fours. Right now she was sitting up, brown eyes intent on getting as much attention as possible.

"She said she worked for which airline?"

"British Airways."

"We might be able to find her through them. Possible, but unlikely. Unless we can get an inside connection." She screwed up her face, thinking hard.

"Ev," Cory sighed deeply. "I hate to admit it, but I don't think Jules wants to be found. She's made no contact with me in a week. Nothing." She raised one hand, fingers circling into a large O. "I didn't really think about it much at the time, but whenever I mentioned seeing her again, she always sidestepped the topic. She wasn't mean or anything. Just —"

"Skillful?" Evelyn's sarcasm was apparent.

Cory felt herself cringing again. The truth hurt. A lot. "Maybe," she admitted.

Evelyn's lips twisted down. "So what you're saying is that she picked you up looking for a weekend fling, knowing all along that it was nothing more than that."

Another sigh escaped Cory as she nodded. "I'm beginning to think so. But what's odd is that we really were quite comfortable with each other, after the first night." Her eyes began to mist as she lifted her gaze to Evelyn. "I really thought we clicked. I mean, there were moments when it felt like we had lived together forever. And I know she enjoyed herself."

Still frowning, Evelyn was puzzled. "But you didn't have sex?"

Cory shook her head. "No. I mean we tried. A few times. Friday night I thought that was all she wanted. But we stopped. *She* stopped when she knew that I was uncomfortable." Her mind wandered back in time. Had it only been a week ago? "Then Saturday night, Sophie started begging for attention, and it kind of ruined the mood."

"What about Sunday?"

She thought about it, finding insight. "You know, Sunday night I was all over her, and she practically pushed me away. Nicely, of course. What's odd, though, is that she made it clear that she wanted to, but then she just held me and we talked for a while. Mostly about Sophie."

Evelyn was nodding. "So it's almost like she knew Sunday night that she wasn't going to see you again."

"Maybe. I just can't believe that I was so stupid. I thought she was so wonderful. I actually believed that it was really the beginning of something special."

"I'm so sorry, Cory. The whole thing just sucks."

Sophie was again demanding attention. She was squirming as she sat, trying to move her hind legs in an effort to stand up.

"Look. I think she's trying to stand!" Cory reached over, helping the pup to her feet. "Come on, sweetie." She scooted herself a couple of feet away as she urged the puppy to take a few steps.

"Come on, Sophie. You can do it." She patted the floor and watched the intelligence in Sophie's eyes. The dog looked at her outstretched hand, then turned her face up to Cory's. Her tail wagged as she made a noise like a strangled bark.

Cory laughed. "I don't think she knows quite how to bark yet," she told Evelyn, then turned back to Sophie.

"Come on, Sophie. Come over here so I can pet you."

Tail wagging, Sophie took her first tentative step, placing first a front paw, then a back paw, forward. Then the other legs followed. Gaining courage, she started all over again, finally finding herself in Cory's arms.

Cory could have cried with sheer joy. "That's my girl," she laughed.

Even Evelyn was touched as she watched her friend receiving puppy kisses all over her face. "At least *one* good thing came out of last weekend," she said. "You got Sophie."

"No, Raymond. Absolutely not." Julia ducked her head, letting one of Raymond's assistants adjust the collar of her dress as he zipped it up from behind.

Backstage was a madhouse. Models and prop people and journalists and photographers were running every which way as the models changed outfits as quickly as possible for their next turn down the runway.

"You have no choice on this one, honey. So don't pull this uppity shit with me." Raymond was gritting his teeth. "I told her you would meet with her briefly after the show."

"Raymond. I will be exhausted by then. The last thing I want to do is talk to some reporter." The assistant was turning her around, adjusting the wig that had gone slightly askew.

"Not *some* reporter. Irene Jacobson from *Vogue*. And she specifically asked to speak with you and Yvonne."

"Why us?" She had become so accustomed to doing these shows that it no longer rattled her to have a complete conversation while she was poked and prodded from all different sides. Someone was lifting her feet, pulling off one shoe and replacing it with another.

Raymond's grin was almost evil. "She said she wanted to talk to the real veterans of the runway."

Julia rolled her eyes. "You are such a prick, Raymond."

"I love you too, doll." He kissed her cheek and adjusted the collar of her dress one more time. "You're next. Get out there and break a leg." He turned on one heel and began walking away. "And don't smile!" he yelled back over his shoulder.

Julia's eyes fell to the overworked assistant who

was kneeling in front of her tucking her foot into yet another shoe. "As if there's any chance of that," she muttered under her breath, then laughed when she heard his harrumph.

Chapter 13

Cory knew it was hopeless, but she wouldn't give up. She kept telling herself that she was a reporter, after all. She should be able to locate Jules. Somehow.

She had started by going to the hotel that Jules had stayed in. She approached the hotel manager, armed with the overnight bag that Jules had left at her apartment. She explained that a guest of his hotel had left the bag and its contents in her car, and asked if he could locate Jules' address so that she could return her belongings.

Annoyed at first, the manager finally capitulated to

Cory's cajoling and began looking through the hotel's records.

"We can look for her address, but I'm afraid I can't give out that information to you. We can contact her and let her know that we have some of her belongings and ask if she'd like us to ship it." He approached the computer in his office and sat down.

"That's okay," Cory told him. "I just hate it that she left all these clothes behind." She didn't like the idea, but thought that once they found her address she might be able to coax it from him anyway.

He sat at the computer, poised and waiting. Cory's cheeks grew red when she told him that she only knew Jules' first name.

He almost snorted. Then he asked if she knew the room number that Jules had stayed in.

Cory searched her memory, kicking herself for not noticing the room number when they'd gone there the week before. "I know it was on the fifth floor."

"This is impossible," the manager told her, irritated.

No amount of coercion or charm would change his mind. "All of our records are by last name and room number," he told her several times.

Knowing nothing more than when she'd arrived, she left with Jules' overnight bag slung over her shoulder.

Next she attempted one phone call after another to British Airways. She tried the main number. Human Resources. Payroll. She tried every ploy imaginable, even pretending to be an old friend looking for someone she hadn't seen in years. Nothing worked. Nobody knew anyone named Jules. Cory was beginning to think that she didn't even exist.

Well over a month passed before she resigned herself to the fact that she would never see Jules again. But just when she felt that the emptiness and frustration would overcome her, she finally began to snap out of it.

Intent on moving ahead and forgetting that the weekend with Jules ever happened, she became single-minded about finding a new home and was nearly desperate when she realized that the task was much more difficult than she'd anticipated. Every landlord that she talked to refused to consider leasing an apartment to anyone with a puppy.

She began searching through the listings for rental houses, quickly becoming discouraged when she discovered that the prices were nowhere near anything she could afford.

The two weeks that Edgar had originally given her to bring Sophie to the office had long since passed. She had been well aware of the deadline but had quietly decided to ignore it. She knew that she wasn't fooling anyone, especially Edgar, when she continued to bring Sophie in with her each day.

Their routine was the same. Every morning, Sophie would obediently curl up under Cory's desk until noon. Then the two of them would go outside for a walk at lunch time. If Cory had an appointment, Sophie went with her. Cory went virtually nowhere without Sophie.

But with December only a few days away, Cory knew she couldn't wait much longer. Pretty soon it would be too cold to go for long walks, and Sophie needed some room where she could run and play.

Late on a Friday afternoon, Cory was looking

forward to a long, exhaustive weekend of phone calls and apartment hunting.

When her phone rang, she tried not to sound nervous when she heard Edgar's voice.

"If you're not in the middle of something I need you to come to my office."

"Right away, Edgar." She was already pushing her chair back.

"And bring your dog," she heard him mutter before the line went dead.

"Uh-oh." She looked down at Sophie and cringed. "This might be it, sweetie. I think the boss is about to give you the boot." She squatted down and flipped open the door to Sophie's crate. "Come on, sweetie."

She stood up, smiling with fondness as Sophie uncurled her growing body and stepped outside of her cage. She stretched several times before falling into step with Cory. They walked the length of the corridor to Edgar's office. The door was open, and Cory was surprised to see that Edgar was sitting in one of the chairs usually reserved for visitors. The chair behind his desk was empty.

He waved her inside, then let his eyes fall to Sophie. She wandered over to him, turning brown eyes up expectantly. Edgar responded by scratching her head.

"She's getting around okay, huh?" Although he spoke to Cory, his attention was fully focused on the dog.

"She's doing great. You'd never know that she ever had any problem. The vet doesn't really want her to run or jump yet, but by the time Christmas is here I'm sure I won't be able to hold her back."

Edgar nodded, smiling. "She's well-behaved. Quiet, too."

Cory nodded, guilt and anxiety growing. She decided to try to head him off.

"Look, I know that she's been coming here a lot longer than the two weeks —"

He raised both hands to cut her off. "If we don't talk about it then we can pretend we forgot, right?"

Cory stared at him dumbly. Then she smiled.

"Sit down," he told her, his voice growing gruff. He shuffled in his seat, uncomfortable. "I just wanted to ask you if you'd found a place yet."

Cory stared at him, not believing that this wasn't a work-related conversation.

"No luck so far," she replied. "Most apartments won't take pets, and the houses are just way out of my price range."

Edgar put a finger inside the neckline of his collar and tugged. Then he pulled at his tie and finally unbuttoned the button at his neck.

"Listen, my wife and I were talking last night," he shifted in his chair. "We've got a place up on the North Shore that our daughters have been staying at off and on for the past few years." He continued to scratch Sophie's head, but was finally looking at Cory. "And, well, Jenny's been gone two years now and Kelly went back to school in September. The place is sitting empty, so if you wanna take a look at it . . ."

Cory didn't know what to say, and Edgar continued. "It's nothing fancy. Needs some work, too. If you're handy." He rubbed the back of his hand across his brow.

"Edgar, it's really sweet of you to offer. But like I said, I really can't afford much."

He waved her off again, pulling himself up and putting on his gruff face. "We wouldn't charge you rent. The place is paid off and just sitting empty like I said. You'd have to pay the heat and electric. But otherwise you'd be doing us a favor by taking care of the place."

Cory couldn't believe it. For a moment it crossed her mind that this house must be a dump. But she decided to reserve judgment. An offer like this was too good to dismiss so readily.

"Wow." She stammered, searching for words. "I don't know what to say."

Edgar shrugged. "Why don't you just go take a look at the place. See if you like it. No strings."

"Sure." The shell shock was beginning to wear off, and Cory was coming to her senses. "Can I see it tomorrow?"

"Nine o'clock okay?"

Cory nodded, and Edgar scribbled the address on a piece of paper and stood up as he handed it to her. He gave Sophie a quick pat on the head as he dismissed them.

Cory was slow to stand, but Sophie was instantly at her side, ready to go.

"See you tomorrow, then," she said awkwardly while they stood face-to-face.

"Nine o'clock," he repeated.

"I'll be there," she replied. "Thanks." She patted her thigh as she turned to leave the office, and Sophie followed close behind.

Chapter 14

The house that Edgar owned was actually in Nahaunt, a small Boston suburb on the North Shore that was technically a tiny island. A single two-lane bridge connected the mainland to the small town that was completely surrounded by the Atlantic Ocean.

Cory had set her expectations low, but when she pulled her car into the driveway, she couldn't quite believe her eyes.

The house was a small Cape Cod–style cottage with wind- and ocean-worn shaker shingles that were so common along the coastal region. While the house had probably seen better days, it was still in exceptional shape. And the view was nothing short of spectacular. The house was situated on the top of a rocky cliff that led out to a short, sand-covered beach. The roar of the ocean pierced her ears as Cory stepped out of the car. The smell of the salt water assaulted her senses.

Even Sophie seemed to respond, sniffing the air and circling the front yard as if she was missing something and just itching to investigate.

They were greeted at the door by a short, middle-aged woman who waved them inside with a wide, toothy smile.

"You must be Cory and Sophie. Come in, come in. Edgar's told me so much about you." She quickly introduced herself as Alma, Edgar's wife, before she squatted down to give Sophie her full attention.

"She's a beautiful dog. Good for you for taking her in and giving her a home. I read your story and was very angry about what that man was doing to those poor dogs."

She straightened up and faced Cory, still smiling. "Our family has always had dogs," she explained, then apologized and offered to make some coffee or tea.

Cory accepted politely. "Don't go to any trouble."

"No trouble. Why don't you take a look around and see if you like the place. I'll be in the kitchen when you're done." Patting Sophie on the head in much the same way that Edgar always did, she smiled again and left the room.

Alone, Cory let her eyes take a long look around the first-floor space. She was still standing in the small entrance way, which opened up into a small but comfortable living room. A blazing fire snapped and crackled in the fireplace on the near wall.

She took a few steps into the living room, noting the floor-to-ceiling bookshelves that lined the entire interior wall to her left. The room was furnished simply, with a couch, a love seat, and a small coffee table.

Trying not to get too excited, she walked past the sofa and stepped into a small dining room. Her eyes went instantly to the wide sliding-glass doors, and she made her way quickly to stare at the view. The doors opened to a small deck that led to the beach and ocean below.

"Wow." Shaking her head, she turned down a short hallway to the stairs that curved back toward the center of the house. She lifted Sophie into her arms, knowing that stairs were off-limits for another month or so.

After climbing the stairs slowly, it didn't take her long to take a quick tour of two bedrooms and a small bathroom. At the far end of the master bedroom was a bay window atop a small window seat. Instantly drawn, Cory again found her eyes looking down at the incredible view of the ocean as it swept over the beach below.

Then she spotted Edgar. He was bending over to pick something up, then turning and throwing it as far down the beach as he could. It took a moment before Cory understood what he was doing. But then she saw them, two great, large dogs, racing headlong down the beach to whatever Edgar had thrown.

A grin pulled at Cory's lips. She finally understood why Edgar had been so lenient and understanding about Sophie. The golden retriever was running neck and neck with the Dalmatian until the golden picked up the stick that Edgar had thrown. The two dogs played tug of war for a moment or two before racing back to Edgar.

Cory gave Sophie a quick hug, her mind already made up. "What do you think, sweetie? Do you want to live here?" She made only a cursory glance in the second bedroom before trotting back down the stairs, anxious to find the kitchen and Edgar's wife.

Cory found herself warming to the older woman instantly. Alma had made hot chocolate and was sitting at the small kitchen table when Cory found her. Cory knew that Alma's enthusiasm was genuine when she told her that she loved the house. Her laughter filled the room as she related stories of the house and the times her family had shared when they had lived there.

"We bought the place about a year after we were married. Then we had the two girls and before long we'd really outgrown it. I'm not quite sure why Ed still hangs on to it. It's beautiful in the summertime. But the winters are quite cold. The windows tend to get drafty, and the only way to keep the chill out is to light a fire."

"He said your daughters stay here off and on?"

The permanent smile lines around Alma's eyes deepened. "They have. But Jenny's been gone for several years. Kelly will be graduating from Tufts in the spring, and she really wants to move out west." She shrugged her shoulders, wistful. "We've talked about selling for so long, but Ed always wants to hold off a little longer. And now he'd love for you to take care of it for a while, if you want to."

Cory didn't know what to say.

"You'd be doing him a favor, dear. He needs an excuse to hang on to this place and his past for a little bit longer."

"I can't believe it." She was embarrassed that he had even offered her such a great deal, and she said so.

Alma reached over and laid a hand over hers as it rested on the tabletop. "I'm sure Edgar is a big old bear at work. But he's got a huge soft spot. I think you remind him a bit of his girls." She took her hand away and laughed. "And maybe you even remind him a bit of himself. He says you're a good writer and a hard worker." She lowered her voice. "And that you've got balls. He likes that." She laughed again. "Then when you brought Sophie in and mentioned that you were looking for a bigger place . . ." She clucked her tongue. "Well, you pretty much found his heart that day."

She leaned back in her chair. "You're right, it's a great deal. We just ask that you take care of the old place."

The ocean air whipped through the kitchen as the back door opened and Edgar stepped inside. There were several moments of chaos as the two full-grown dogs discovered Sophie. As the dogs barked and ran circles around one another, Edgar raised his voice and called out to Cory.

"What do you think?"

With a quick glance at Alma, Cory's face nearly broke as she smiled. "I love it. Can I still take it?"

Edgar's nod was curt. "It's yours."

Cory didn't miss the secretive smile on Alma's lips.

Chapter 15

Within days, Cory was completely moved in. By the time the holidays had arrived, both she and Sophie were completely settled and thriving.

"I don't suppose you've heard from that woman yet," Evelyn asked Cory on her first visit to Cory's new home. She had toured the house and helped Cory unpack. Now they sat together in the living room before the fire that Cory was stoking.

"Who?" Grimacing, Cory feigned ignorance.

"You know who. That Jules woman."

"Nope. Not a word," Cory sighed.

"I'm sorry, Cory."

"Thanks, but I'm okay." *Almost,* she told herself. *I'm almost there.*

"Have you stopped trying to find her?"

Cory nodded. "When we moved in here. It just seems so silly to keep trying. And I got sick of feeling sorry for myself."

Evelyn laughed. "Good for you. So are you ready to move on? I know someone I want you to meet. Her name's Tanya. She'll be at my place on New Year's Eve. Will you come?"

Cory groaned, but Evelyn worked her magic and charm, finally convincing her that she wouldn't be sorry.

Cory gave herself a once-over in the mirror. Her heart just wasn't in this New Year's Eve thing. Her hair was misbehaving badly, refusing to stay put and falling forward despite all her efforts.

Sophie seemed to know that something was up, and she kept making circles around and between Cory's legs, looking for attention.

Unable to put it off any longer, she picked up her car keys and was nearly out the door when the phone rang. It was Evelyn.

She was giggling, and Cory suspected that her friend was already dipping into the liquor meant for the evening. She wasn't mistaken.

"I don't think we have enough champagne for tonight," Evelyn told her.

"I don't suppose that's because you've already cracked open a bottle," Cory teased.

"Of course not. I'm saving it for midnight. Anyway, I wanted to ask if you'd stop off and pick up a couple of bottles for me. Do you mind?" Music played in the background, and Cory checked her watch. It was only seven. Were people there already?

"No problem." She was actually relieved to be able to legitimately put off walking in that door. She had no desire to meet *Tanya*, or whatever her name was.

"Will you pick up some chips and salsa, too?" Evelyn asked sweetly.

Cory laughed. "Anything else?"

"Just you." Evelyn dropped her voice to a whisper. "Tanya just got here, and she looks hot. She can't wait to meet you."

Now Cory rolled her eyes.

"I'll see you soon, Ev. Bye." She hung up the phone and gave Sophie a quick pat on the head. "I won't be late," she promised, then opened the door.

The liquor store six blocks from Evelyn's house was completely out of chips and salsa. So after spending nearly thirty minutes in line to pay for the champagne, Cory found herself next door at the grocery market.

She almost choked when she got to the checkout counter. At least a dozen people were in front of her. As she began railing inside at all the last-minute shoppers who should have been better prepared, she had to laugh at herself. Wasn't she a last-minute shopper too? She decided that Evelyn would pay dearly.

Distributing the four bags of chips and two jars of salsa equally to both arms, she settled herself in for the long wait ahead.

The woman two people ahead of her was hurriedly

flipping through one of the gossip rags. *Probably trying to get to the good stuff before it's her turn.* The woman was browsing through an article that proclaimed that an alien baby was born to a famous guitarist in Australia.

Cory tried not to roll her eyes, deciding that it probably wasn't very polite to be reading over someone's shoulders.

As everyone in line shuffled one foot forward, Cory's eyes fell to the rest of the magazines that lined the rack in front of the counter.

She read each title, noting that she had probably never picked up any one of them before. Except *TV Guide*, of course. But she didn't even recognize the faces on the cover. *Not much to look at there.*

She barely recognized the faces on most of the magazines, and she contemplated whether or not she really should be keeping up better with current affairs.

The President and his wife smiled and waved from the White House lawn on the cover of *Time*. *People* was celebrating its twenty-five most interesting people of the year. Cory wrinkled her nose at all of the fashion magazines that followed, one after another, with headlines like "How to lose those extra pounds in the New Year" and "How to make your husband happy."

"Give me a break," Cory muttered with distaste. She moved on to the headline of the next magazine. "How old is too old? An inside look at the aging fashion industry."

Okay, that's not so bad, she thought, her eyes focusing on the smiling face that adorned the cover. She was quite pretty, actually, with auburn curls cascading down her neck and eyes that were the most interesting shade of . . . *violet?*

Cory felt her knees go weak. Then a strangled moan that came from her own lips replaced the rushing sound in her ears. Two bags of chips hit the tiled floor before her hand could curl around the magazine.

Heart pounding, she picked up the errant chips and tried to juggle them in her arms while she stared at the face that she was certain she knew.

Jules.

"Next!"

It can't be her. She continued to stare, her eyes no longer aligning with her memory. The hair was the wrong color. And she didn't think that Jules's cheekbones were so pronounced. She was mistaken. *I must still have it bad. Christ, next I'll be seeing her on TV.*

"Move it, lady!"

The voice from behind her brought her back to reality, and she was embarrassed to find that everyone in the place was waiting for her. She dumped her purchases on the counter and reached back to put the magazine on the rack.

But those eyes. Thinking better of it, she tossed the magazine on top of the jars of salsa and reached for her wallet.

Once in the car, she pulled out of the parking lot and made her way quickly down the six blocks to Evelyn's house. She drove past the house, swearing when she couldn't find a single empty spot to pull into. She ended up nearly eight houses down before she could finally pull over.

Damn! Her hands were still shaking. *Like a woman that I spent the weekend with is on the cover of* Vogue. *Right.*

Taking a deep breath to steady herself, she cut the engine and pushed the door open. Reaching for the bags of groceries and champagne, she stopped cold when she saw the face again.

That's her. I know it.

Tossing the magazine to the passenger seat, she grabbed the bags and tumbled out of the car, her mind racing as she climbed over a pile of snow to get to the sidewalk.

Her intentions were clear. *Get in. Get out. Avoid both Evelyn and the Tanya woman, if I can.*

Music was pounding from the living room as she entered through the back door and deposited her purchases on the kitchen counter. She emptied the bags quickly and was reaching for the doorknob when Evelyn appeared, giggling, with a bottle of beer in one hand and a long, unlit cigar in the other.

"Cory! Where have you been?"

Cory was shuffling her feet fast. "The lines were hell. You should see the place."

Evelyn eyed that hand that held the doorknob. "Where are you going?" Her eyes narrowed. "Tanya's waiting for you."

"Ev, I gotta go."

Evelyn's face went hard. "Don't do this, Cory."

"Evelyn, I swear. Something came up. I have to leave." She wiped one hand across her brow. "I'll call you tomorrow, I promise."

"Cory! You little shit!" The last word hit Cory's ears just as she slammed the door behind her.

She drove home with a purpose, her mind spinning with the possibilities of finding Jules. Once home, she greeted Sophie and took her for a quick walk outside before settling the two of them on the couch, the magazine in Cory's lap.

She stared at the cover again before flipping to the table of contents and then turning the pages quickly to the article.

"How old is too old? A look at the aging of our fashion industry," by Irene Jacobson. She let her eyes wander quickly to the photos on the opening spread. But none of the images were of the woman on the cover. Maybe she'd been mistaken. Maybe the photo had nothing to do with this article.

Then she turned the page. Her breath caught in her throat as she stared at the photograph of the woman who had eluded her. This was definitely Jules. She was leaning forward and wearing a strapless dress. A slight twinkle was in her eyes as she lifted her lips in a smile. Her hair was pulled back away from her face in a long, single braid. Smooth, square shoulders tipped provocatively. Cory would recognize those shoulders anywhere. And the way her hair was pulled back made it seem shorter, and darker.

"Dammit." Finding her voice, Cory swore under her breath while she tried to steady her jittery nerves. Her journalist's eye looked for the photo credit. *Julia Westgate. Photo by Armanda.*

"Julia. Jules." She shook her head slowly, once again feeling foolish for having been so easily duped.

She turned to the next page and the next, finding

the end of the article. But there were no other pictures of Jules. Cory turned back to the beginning, her eyes scanning the article.

The story focused mainly on the growing number of models who seemed to slip from sight after the age of forty. The author noted the few exceptions that she had found, but the rest of the article tried to draw a parallel between the discarding of older models and society's — the buying public's in particular — valuing of young faces over the old.

With the exception of a few quotes from various sources, the article was mostly narrative. There was only one quote from Julia Westgate: "When asked whether or not she felt there was age discrimination within the industry, fashion model Julia Westgate had little comment. 'I don't know whether or not I would call it discrimination, but yes, things do change in the business as you get older.' "

"It's not her." Evelyn returned the magazine to the table.

"I'm telling you, it is. I was with her for an entire weekend."

Evelyn was frowning, concern showing in the crease between her brows. "Cory. Honey," she sighed. "Look, I know you fell bad for this woman. And I know how badly you'd like to find her. But this isn't her. I saw her, remember?"

Cory opened her mouth and then quickly clamped it tight, biting back her protest. The look on Evelyn's face said that she thought that Cory had really gone over the deep end.

"Honey, I'm worried about you. You've got to let go of this woman, for your own good."

Cory spent nearly the entire weekend doing searches on the Internet, finding more photos of Julia Westgate than she would have thought possible. Every new image either confirmed or denied her certainty that Julia and Jules were the same.

Exhausted, she finally turned off the computer and curled up with Sophie on the couch. "How can I prove that it's her without sounding like a complete psycho?" she was looking at Sophie as she spoke, nearly expecting her dog to have the answer.

Sophie was lifting a paw and laying it on Cory's thigh. Cory absently rubbed the growing puppy's head while she stared into the brown eyes. Then it came to her.

"Idiot!" she shouted, jumping off the couch and reaching for the telephone. "Why didn't I think of this before?" She was giddy from the rush of adrenaline that ran through her.

She had to search her memory for a moment before remembering the phone number of her friend. Then she punched in the numbers and waited impatiently.

"Hello?"

"Deb? It's Cory."

"Hi. What's up? How's Sophie?"

"She's doing great. I need to bring her by sometime soon." Cory felt a pang of guilt. She hadn't kept her promise very well.

"You should. We'd love to see her." Deb paused.

"So what's up? I haven't heard from you in a while. I missed you at Evelyn's party the other night."

"Yeah. Sorry about that. Something came up . . ." she left the sentence unfinished. "Listen, Deb. I need your help."

"Sure. What's up?"

"I know it's kind of a silly question," she began. "But when Jules and I were there picking up Sophie, do you happen to remember whether Jules paid with a credit card?"

If Deb thought the question odd, she didn't show it. "Yep. She charged everything."

Cory felt herself go weak. "Then I have another favor to ask," she said cautiously.

"Why am I not liking this?" Deb responded to the sound in Cory's voice.

"Because it's kind of sticky. I need to know if there's any way that you can go back and check to see what the name was on the credit card." Cory held her breath while she listened to the silence on the other end.

"This feels unethical," Deb finally responded.

You're this close, Cory told herself, trying to remain calm. "Deb, I wouldn't ask if it wasn't really important."

"Cory, even if I wanted to help, I wouldn't know where to start. That was three months ago."

Cory bit her lip, searching for some kind of story, something to make Deb understand how important that name was. She came up with nothing, then finally settled for the truth. She related the story briefly, leaving out the part about the magazine cover.

"So what will you do if you have her name?"

Cory hadn't even thought about that. "I'm not

sure, really. I haven't thought about it yet," she answered honestly. "I guess I just need to know. That's all."

Deb tried her best to avoid Cory's pleas, finally caving in the end.

"I'll try. But I'm not promising anything," she groaned. "Just be thankful that I'm a hopeless romantic. And bring Sophie by sometime so we can see her."

"I will, Deb. Thanks." Hope was soaring.

Each day passed with Cory convincing herself to wait one more day before calling Deb. Then she decided that if she didn't hear from her by the end of the week, she and Sophie were going on a little visit.

But they didn't have to. Deb's voice greeted Cory from her answering machine on Thursday when she came home from work.

"I found it, Cory. Got a pen?"

But Cory didn't need to find a pen. She already knew the name.

"No name. Just initials. J. A. Westgate. Got that? Hope it works out for you. You owe me, kid."

"Julia Westgate." Cory said the name aloud. For a moment her heart soared. Then she came quickly down to earth. She finally knew for certain who Jules really was, but what was she going to do with the information?

She had no intention of tracking her down. Or did she? She thought about boarding a plane and searching her out. But for what? Where would that get her?

Jules had never had any intention of seeing her beyond that weekend. So what did Cory expect to hear if she saw her face-to-face? What did she want? An apology?

Cory groaned aloud, grimacing. There was no point to it. She had to let this go. She had to. Somehow she had to get on with her life and forget about Jules.

She wandered over to the couch and plopped down, throwing both arms around Sophie and curling up beside her. Enough was enough.

"Someday this will all just be a really good story that I can entertain my friends with."

Sophie just looked at her without lifting her head.

"Maybe I should give that Tanya woman a call. What do you think, Soph?" She scratched Sophie's ears and waited for an answer.

Chapter 16

"Okay, listen up everybody. We've got a lot to get through, so let's get to it." Edgar was displaying his usual grumpy Monday morning charm.

Cory was as guilty as everyone else in the room was. No one seemed interested in beginning the workweek as they chatted about what they'd done over the weekend.

Winter had given way to springtime in New England. Two weeks ago everyone had been bundled up in overcoats and gloves. Today was only the first of

April, and those same people were wearing short-sleeve shirts.

"We've got very little hard news this week." He let a smile drift across the room. "Looks like the nice weather's keeping everyone out of trouble."

Cory tried a halfhearted smile when he glanced her way. The truth was, she didn't want to be there either. Spring fever had hit her hard the past weekend. She had spent a fortune at the garden shop, and now she could think only about the small packets of seeds lined up in her kitchen and the garden plot she would turn.

"Okay. Fire last night in Chelsea. Tom, it's yours." Edgar handed the assignment sheet across the desk to Tom's awaiting hand.

"We've got someone down at the statehouse making noise about the vendors out at Fenway Park. Who wants it?"

George Davis raised a hand, receiving an assignment sheet for his efforts.

"I need someone over at the Common. We need the annual spring photos of tourists in the swan boats." He paused and looked around. "Anyone?"

Nobody wanted this one.

"I need a writer and a photographer." He almost laughed as everyone in the room avoided his stare. "Okay, then. Bill, Janet, it's yours."

Two groans were heard among a number of sighs of relief.

"Okay. I need a reporter and a photographer down on the Cape on Friday." All faces were on him, eyes eager. "A bunch of European models are going to be down there all day filming some kind of travel advertisement."

A few groans surfaced and all eyes were averted. Except Cory's.

"Anyone?"

"I'll take it." Cory barely heard her own voice above the rushing sound in her ears. She cleared her throat, then repeated the words. "I'll take it."

"Heard you the first time, kid." There were only a few snickers. "Bill, you can go with her."

"Lucky me," Bill chirped. "I get tourists, swan boats, and models all in one week."

"Be careful," Edgar grinned. "You don't know what else I might have on this list."

Everyone laughed, and no one caught the vacant stare that blanketed Cory's face. How was she ever going to make it through the week?

It took every ounce of reserve for Cory to contain herself and act as if this were just another assignment. She knew it was a long shot. And she didn't really believe for a moment that Jules would be on the Cape. All she knew was that she had to be there, just in case.

If she seemed preoccupied on the drive down to the Cape, Bill didn't appear to notice. He entertained himself and Cory with horror stories about some of the assignments he'd been on in the past.

They arrived in Hyannis just after noon and found the convergence of models, handlers, and photographers on the beach near a large mound of rocks outside of a small, weathered clam shack.

Leaving Sophie in the car, Cory approached the chaos cautiously while Bill unpacked his equipment.

Spring may have arrived in Boston, but it must have been at least twenty degrees cooler on the Cape. A light wind shifted, sending shivers through Cory and making her glad for the light jacket she wore.

She let her eyes survey the scene before her, trying to make out everything that was happening and picking out the key people for interviews. At least that's what she told herself. The truth was, she was scouring the crowd of faces for one familiar one. But she was quickly disappointed. If Jules was here, she wasn't to be included in this particular shoot.

She spied the person who she assumed must be the director. He was a lean, blond man dressed casually in hiking boots and a lightweight yellow parka. He was speaking in animated tones with two photographers as he stressed the look that he was going for in this particular session.

Four models, clad only in the skimpiest of bathing suits, waited on the large rock formation. They shivered as the ocean waves swept in and sprayed water all over them.

"Shit, Raymond!" Cory's eyes were drawn to a dark-skinned woman who shivered uncontrollably. "We're freezing out here. Let's get the shot over with."

Cory felt Bill's presence as he joined her and began setting up his tripod and other equipment. He had pulled on a heavier jacket as well.

"Did you hear that?" Cory asked under her breath. "I can't believe how cold it is out here."

Bill shrugged and wiped his sleeve across his nose. "I've got news for you, sweetheart," he drawled. "If they were paying me the kind of money that those models are making, I'd strip down to my skivvies and stand out there all day." He put an eye to the viewfinder of his camera and began clicking away.

Cory had to admit that she would probably do the same, but she still couldn't help but sympathize with the models' obvious discomfort. She didn't have to sympathize for long, however. Within a few moments, the director was calling out, "It's a wrap. Take twenty minutes while we set up the next shot."

Then he walked a short distance to join a short, red-headed woman who was standing behind the photographers, observing.

Cory recognized Enid Goldman beneath the long coat and sunglasses. Enid was the marketing director for Regency Travel, the largest travel agency in Boston.

"Bingo," Cory said quietly, for Bill's ears only. "There's my interview."

He lifted his head long enough to follow her gaze, then clucked his tongue. "Good luck. Enid can be a real bitch."

"Yeah, but how can she turn down free advertising?"

"Not to mention your tremendous charm and good looks." Bill grinned and winked. She put a quick elbow to his rib cage, then pulled a tape recorder from her pocket. She checked to make sure it was ready before returning it to her pocket and pulling out a small spiral notebook and a pen.

"Wish me luck." She took a deep breath, steadying her nerves as she stepped forward. It continued to amaze her that she got such jitters before each interview.

* * * * *

Arms folded, Julia stood just inside the doorway of the models' trailer, her face just inches from the pane of the glass. Her heart was pounding.

She had thought she had prepared herself for the moment when she would see Cory again. But this wasn't quite the way she had planned it in her mind.

It hadn't really been a conscious choice, but rather an inevitable one. The fantasies had never stopped. The daydreams of seeing Cory, of explaining everything to her, of apologizing and asking for another chance.

But the uncertainty of Cory's response had kept her at bay, kept her on the other side of the ocean where she wouldn't have to face Cory's rejection.

She still couldn't identify what it was that was different about the weekend with Cory. Maybe it had something to do with her age. Perhaps her growing disenchantment with her life. Maybe it was simply that Cory had touched her heart.

But she knew that her restlessness was growing. She knew that it was time to let go of the career and life she'd known so long and start fresh with something new. Regardless of what happened with Cory, she was ready to move on. And maybe, just maybe, things would work out with Cory.

Julia had already made arrangements to spend the rest of the week in Boston and had planned to show up on Cory's doorstep and beg her forgiveness.

How ironic that it should happen like this instead. "Damn," she cursed under her breath.

She didn't want their first meeting to be in front

of the entire crew. She didn't want Raymond's watchful eyes to spoil their reunion.

Her lips twisted as she watched Cory speaking to the producer of the shoot, just two feet away from Raymond's ears. *If only he knew . . .*

She felt panic rising at the thought of stepping outside the trailer. She thought through the schedule for the day and knew that it would be at least another hour before she was called out for her turn on the beach. Maybe Cory would be gone by then. After all, it was a rather tedious experience, just a lot of standing around, watching and waiting.

She started the inevitable scripting in her mind, playing out their encounter if Cory was still there later in the afternoon. Then she shivered, not liking any of the ways that the scenario played out.

"This is not good," she whispered. "Not good at all."

Bill was getting impatient, and bored. Cory tried to appear engrossed in what was going on, ignoring his sighs and the way he shifted his weight from side to side.

"I think I've got all the shots I need," he finally told her. "Are you about ready to head out?"

She bit her lip for a moment before replying.

"I don't think I've got enough material yet. I thought I'd hang around until they're finished and see if I can get something out of the director."

Bill didn't respond at first. She refused to meet his gaze, and instead tried to appear distracted by the activity around her. They had just called for another break. Surely this couldn't go on much longer.

"Uh, Cory," he began quietly, trying to keep the sarcasm from his voice. "This isn't exactly an investigative story. It's a fluff piece. We've got pictures and quotes. That's enough."

She tried not to get irritated. After all, under other circumstances she would have been in the car and on her way already. She turned her eyes briefly to his.

"I really just want to get one more quote, Bill."

He stared at her, eyes speaking volumes. "How about if I put my equipment away and take Sophie for a walk up the beach. Would that be okay?"

Relieved, she pulled the car keys from her jacket pocket and dropped them into his palm. "That would be great. Just don't let her off the leash though. I don't quite trust her not to run yet."

Bill nodded and disappeared behind the sand dunes without another word.

Julia was taking deep breaths, her mind made up. There was no other way. When she stepped outside, she simply would not let her eyes meet Cory's. It was that simple. It was a gamble, though. But she didn't really think that Cory was the type of woman who would interrupt the shoot by making a scene. No, Cory would hang back, she was sure.

Just don't look at her, Julia repeated the words again and again. Then with another deep breath, she turned the knob and pushed the door open.

* * * * *

Cory knew without looking that it was Jules. She couldn't explain why, but she knew.

She turned to her right, bracing for the blow she knew would come. And there she was. Not even fifty yards away. The woman whom she hadn't thought she would ever lay eyes on again.

Cory could barely breathe as her heart began to pound wildly. Julia, walking toward the photographers, was wrapped in a white terry-cloth bathrobe, bare ankles exposed with each step across the sand.

She looked quite different from the last time Cory had seen her. Her hair was much longer, nearly to her shoulders, and was a light auburn color. The sunlight danced off the curls that the wind picked up and swirled around. And she wore makeup. Lots of it. Not the simple lipstick that she had worn that weekend.

Cory thought she was nothing short of exquisite.

She realized that her legs were shaking uncontrollably, and she let herself drop down and sit on the beach, trying to cross her legs casually.

Julia was speaking with the photographer and the director. Or rather, they were speaking to her. She was nodding and holding one hand above her eyes to shade the sunlight as she looked in the direction they were pointing.

Two other models, dressed in similar robes, joined them, and the three quickly moved and positioned themselves in front of the small, weather-beaten shack.

Cory couldn't take her eyes from her as she spoke to her silently, willing Julia to look her way. But Julia seemed to be the consummate professional, her eyes focused squarely on the photographer as his shutter snapped away. She moved when told to. Bent just this way when she was directed, all the while not once breaking her steady focus on the photographer.

"Wrap it up. Thanks, girls. You can go home now."

Just like that is was over. Caught off guard, it took several seconds for Cory to scramble to her feet. She had to catch Jules before she went back inside the trailer.

"Whoa!" Bill grabbed her shoulder, and she pulled away from him violently. "Where are you going?"

Cory's eyes never left Julia. She had to get down there. Fast. "I just need ten minutes. Meet me at the car." She called the last few words over her shoulder as she sprinted across the sand.

Her eyes followed the back of Julia's head, just a few steps from the trailer.

"Jules!" She hadn't intended to call out her name.

Julia's hand was reaching for the door.

"Jules!" *Almost there. Almost there.*

The door was open, and Julia disappeared inside.

Any semblance of pride was gone by the time she reached the door. Sucking air deep into her lungs, Cory raised a fist and began to knock.

"Jules." She said the name again, quieter this time.

"Excuse me. Can I help you with something?"

Startled, Cory turned toward the voice that belonged to the dark blond man who she had assumed to be the director. He was looking down at her with a smile on his face, his fingers tracing the outline of his goatee.

"No. Yes. Well, maybe." Cory laughed and tried to catch her breath. "I just wanted to talk to Jules — er, Julia."

The expression on the man's face didn't change. The smile remained.

"Ah. You must be a fan?"

"No." Cory felt confused. How could she explain? "I'm a friend, actually. Maybe you could tell her that I'm here?"

Raymond's eyes narrowed. He let his gaze wander the length of her body, and his anger flared.

"A friend. Really? And how long have you known Julia?" *A friend, my ass,* Raymond thought. *This is one of Julia's discarded flings. Dammit, if I have to bail her out again . . .*

Cory calculated the time. "About seven months or so," she told him, then wondered why in hell she was telling him anything.

Raymond considered this while he decided which tact to take. He put a finger to his lips and drew himself up.

"So you're a groupie, of sorts."

Cory's heart went cold. *What in the hell is this guy talking about?*

"Look. My name is Cory. Just tell Julia that I'm here."

Raymond threw back his head, his laughter harsh. When his eyes met Cory's they were focused and smoldering.

"Listen, sweetie," he dropped his voice down, each word pronounced in a distinct, clipped fashion. "It doesn't matter what your name is. She doesn't want to see you."

Cory was steaming. "I don't know who the fuck you think you are —"

"I'm her manager." He cut her off neatly. "And I can't tell you how many women I've had to stop at her doorstep."

Cory stared at him, unblinking.

119

"Do you think for one moment that you're anything special to her? What did you share? A night? A weekend?" He folded his arms, looking down his nose with disdain. "You are one in a hundred, dear."

Cory continued to stare. "I don't believe you." Her words sounded lifeless.

"Oh no? Has she ever called you? Tried to contact you? Did she even tell you her real name?" He raised a fine brow, noting with pleasure that he had hit the right target.

Cory stared at him, blinking hard. *He knows everything*. She stepped backward. She couldn't think straight, and breathing was becoming difficult.

One in a hundred . . . The words repeated themselves again and again. *One in a hundred.*

Her mind went to the woman inside the trailer, and Cory wondered what she must be thinking. *She must have heard me calling her name. But she ignored me. She must be in there right now thanking her manager for keeping me away.*

What a fool!

Cory turned and ran. As fast as she could. Up the sandy slope to the dunes, to Bill, to her car, and to Sophie.

Chapter 17

Julia didn't get it. She had escaped to her trailer just in time, moving quickly to the bedroom and away from the windows. She didn't want to risk Cory seeing her looking outside.

She had heard Cory calling her, and it had taken everything inside her to ignore her aching heart and keep marching forward to the trailer.

But she was surprised Cory had given up so easily. She'd only knocked once. But she supposed it was better this way. At least now she could show up in Boston, go to Cory's apartment, and plead ignorance.

At least Cory didn't know that she had been watching her all day.

The cold was finally seeping in, and she hugged herself, shivering, before opening a suitcase and pulling out thick wool stockings. She slipped them on and pulled off the bathrobe, quickly stepping into a pair of sweats and pulling a matching sweatshirt over her head.

What would she say to Cory? She realized she'd been staring off into space for some time when she saw the sneaker that she held in one hand. Shaking herself, she slipped on her shoes. She heard a tap at the bedroom door.

She froze. How had Cory gotten inside?

Then the door opened and Raymond stepped inside. He leaned against the doorjamb, a satisfied smirk on his face as he crossed his arms.

"Just thought I'd let you know that I saved your ass again today." He lifted a hand and made a grand show of examining his nails.

"What now?" Julia was not in the mood. Not today.

He drew out the silence, enjoying the way it made her stew. "One of your girlfriends showed up a bit ago, pounding on your door." He let his eyes flutter up to see if he could gauge her reaction. "She was here all afternoon. I'm surprised you didn't spot her."

Julia kept her poise, nonchalantly reaching for a jacket to slip over her shoulders.

"What did you say to her?" she asked.

He met her eyes squarely, lips curling. "The truth. That she was just one of a hundred or so affairs that you've enjoyed over the years and that you wanted nothing to do with her again."

"You said *what?*" Something close to rage engulfed her.

Raymond shrugged. "I was quite brilliant. She actually ran away!" He clapped his hands together. "No need to thank me, dear. It's what I'm here for."

"You son of a bitch! How dare you!" Julia was barely controlling herself. She closed her eyes, imagining Cory's reaction as she suffered the brunt of Raymond's words.

He was confused by her response. He had expected her thanks. But he recovered quickly.

"How dare I, indeed. You know better than to let one of those girls show up here."

Something finally snapped. Years of tension and rage and frustration exploded. "Fuck you, Raymond. I'll have whoever I damn well please in my life, whether you like it or not," she screamed.

"Not as long as you want to work in this business, you won't," he replied smugly, enjoying the exchange, enjoying his dominance.

Julia covered the steps between until she was inches from his face. "Then let me say this so that you understand it clearly, Raymond. I am sick to death of this business. Sick of it and sick of you running my life. I quit. Do you understand?" She was leaning closer. "I quit!"

For the first time since he'd known Julia, he was actually a bit frightened of her. But he held his gaze and his voice, steady.

"I can make sure you never work again."

Now Julia laughed. It was a bitter sound, close to hysteria. But she wasn't hysterical. She was perhaps more lucid than she had been in years.

"You didn't hear me, Raymond. I quit. I'm resigning. *Finis*. No more." She danced away and began to zip up her bag.

"Stop it, Julia." Raymond's voice was grave. "No more games. You're scaring me."

"You're right, Raymond." Her eyes strayed only long enough to see if she was missing anything. "No more games." She looked at him, knowing that he no longer had any power over her, feeling freedom for the first time in her life.

"Isn't it grand?" Her smile was bright and genuine as she tried to step around him. "Now if you'll excuse me, I believe I'll have to call a taxi. Unless I can catch a ride with someone."

Stupefied, he allowed her to pass. Too late he realized that she had gotten by. By the time he caught up with her, he saw that she was speaking with Enid Goldman herself.

"Checkmate," he said under his breath. Julia knew that he would never make a scene in front of a client. He watched as she lifted her bag and slipped it over her shoulder. Then she turned, just long enough to lift a hand in a mocking wave.

"Take care, Raymond," she called, not waiting for a reply.

Raymond gritted his teeth and worked his jaw mightily as he stared after the one person who had been constant in his life for the past twenty years.

Cory had never felt such humiliation. The only saving grace was that thankfully no one had witnessed her exchange with Julia's manager.

As she curled up by the fireplace with Sophie that

124

evening, she contemplated picking up the phone to call Evelyn. But if she talked to Evelyn, she reasoned she would have to admit to everything. It was one thing to guess and assume that Jules had intentionally set her up that weekend. But it was another thing entirely to know that it was true.

She kept hearing that pompous son of a bitch's cruel laughter, and the humiliation kept washing over her.

Chapter 18

Back in her hotel room in Boston, Julia's mind was set. After a quick shower and a change of clothes, she asked the concierge to call for a taxi.

When the car pulled up she slipped inside and leaned forward to talk to the driver.

"I don't have an address, but I can give you directions to where I'm going. Is that all right with you?"

"Lady, as long as you're paying, I'll drive you anywhere you want to go." He put the car in gear and waited for Julia's directions.

"We have to get on the turnpike, I believe. And

it's the second exit. After Cambridge." She wasn't certain of this, but she knew she would recognize the exit when she saw it.

"You headed to Watertown?" The cabbie asked.

The name was familiar, and Julia smiled. "Yes, I believe so. I'll know it when I see it."

"Okay, lady," he said as he pulled the car out into traffic. Julia felt goose bumps rise along her spine. Finally. She was going to see Cory.

It was nearly eight o'clock when the cab driver dropped her off in front of Cory's apartment. Julia had recognized it immediately, delighted by her good memory. She approached the door with trepidation, taking deep breaths as she raised a closed hand and knocked on the door.

She waited nearly a minute, but no one came to the door. She pressed the doorbell. Once. Twice. Then waited. Still no one appeared.

"Just my luck. She's not even in."

Julia looked out at the street, uncertain what to do next. Then, reasoning that she had come an awfully long way just to sit in her hotel room, she stepped to the front of the porch and crouched down on the stoop.

I'll just wait right here. She must be coming home soon.

But as minutes turned slowly into hours, Julia was at a complete loss. It was ten o'clock, and Cory still wasn't home.

She was probably upset and went to a friend's house, she reasoned. Then the thought struck her. *What if she's with her lover?*

Panic rose inside her. She'd never considered that Cory might have a lover now. The thought made her

127

stomach ache, and she doubled over, trying to get control of her emotions.

Forget about whether she has a lover. What makes me think she would ever forgive me for the way I treated her? She began a dialogue in her mind.

She will forgive me, she told her negative side. *If she feels anything for me like I feel for her, she'll forgive me. If she loves me the way I love her . . .*

"Ah!" The single syllable escaped her lips as she realized what she was saying, what she was thinking.

"Bah! Humbug!" She insisted aloud, the negative, sensible side taking over. *I barely know her! I don't believe in love at first sight. Or love at first anything . . .*

She listened to the voices in her head, playing both sides, until a small smile crept to her lips and warmth filled her heart. She felt what she felt, and she knew what she knew. "I can call it whatever I like," she whispered.

Now if only Cory would come home so we can get on with it . . .

She waited for another half hour before giving up. Reluctantly, she stood and stretched, then made her way to the sidewalk for the walk up the street to the intersection, remembering the last time she had taken this exact same path.

Chapter 19

Julia was torn. The more time that passed, the more uncertain she became. While the first morning light found her more determined than ever to talk things over with Cory, she was even more fearful of Cory's reaction.

Unable to sleep in, Julia found her way to the resaurant in the hotel for a quick cup of coffee. She convinced herself that she would miss Cory if she didn't get to the apartment at the crack of dawn. So she was outside and climbing into a cab before the city began to yawn.

Cory's neighborhood was completely quiet when Julia approached the apartment. She glanced around the neighborhood, noting the silence that blanketed the street, and hesitated before ringing the doorbell.

She stood on the doorstep, staring hard at the three panes of glass in the door, and waited.

Her heart rose when she saw the doorknob turn and the door swing open. Then it fell hard, along with her jaw, as she stared at the sight before her.

A young man, dressed only in boxer shorts and T-shirt, was peering at her through half-closed lids.

In that moment of confusion, Julia wondered how she could have ended up at the wrong house. She looked quickly up and down the street until she was nearly certain that she was at the right place.

Maybe it's her brother, she thought. *Good god, it might be worse than I thought. Maybe she's gone straight!*

"Um, hullo," she finally began. "I'm looking for Cory."

"Who?" The young man asked groggily.

"Cory Hayes?"

He stared at her dumbly. "You got the wrong place. She doesn't live here." He started to close the door, but Julia held out her hand to keep it from closing.

"Wait a minute. I know she lives here. I was here with her just a few months ago."

"Oh." His eyes finally opened wide. "I just moved in back in January. I think she lived here before me. I still get mail for her now and then."

Julia felt panic rising.

"She's moved? Do you have her new address?"

He shook his head, brushing the back of his hand against the stubble on his chin.

"Sorry," he said. "I don't know anything about her."

She didn't stop him when he closed the door. Instead, she turned and stared out at the houses that lined the street.

Now what am I going to do? The only thing she really knew about Cory that might help is that she worked for the newspaper. If she waited until Monday she could probably find her there. But the thought of walking into her place of employment seemed less than desirable. Besides, she would go crazy wandering around the city for two days, waiting and wondering what was going to happen.

She left the porch and started walking. There was one other place that she could try, but this time she didn't have a clue about how to get there.

"This is becoming a habit." She smiled wryly as she hailed yet another taxi.

They drove to two other animal shelters before finally ending up at the one where Cory had adopted Sophie. When they pulled into the parking lot, Julia wasted no time. After asking the driver to wait for her, she went inside and looked around.

The first thing she noticed was that it was much quieter than the last time she'd been there. No one was in the front office at all, and so she waited impatiently for someone to notice she was there.

Moments later, Deb opened the door that led to the kennels and greeted Julia with a smile.

"Hullo," Julia returned the greeting, and Deb did a double take. *Well, I'll be damned.*

"We've met before, haven't we? Aren't you Cory's friend?" She asked the questions lightly, feigning casualness.

131

Julia smiled with relief. It felt good to hear someone else say Cory's name.

"Yes. I'm Julia Westgate." She held out her hand, enjoying the freedom of saying her own name.

Deb shook her hand briefly. "It's good to see you again. What can we do for you?" She moved behind the counter, holding Julia's gaze. "I don't suppose you're here to adopt a new pet?"

"No," Julia chuckled, then stopped herself when she realized that she might soon be able to do just that. The thought sent a shiver down her back. "But maybe soon. You never know."

"Well we have plenty here whenever you're ready," Deb told her.

"I'll keep that in mind." Julia continued to smile as her voice became conspiring. "Actually, I have an ulterior motive for being here. I just got into town last night and went by Cory's place to surprise her. But it seems that she's moved. I was hoping you might know her new address, or how I might reach her."

Deb was in a dilemma. She hadn't talked with Cory in over a month. And she hadn't asked Cory about Julia in several months. As far as she knew, Cory had never done anything with the information that she'd given her, but she wasn't certain.

"Gee, I really wish I could help. But I really don't know her new address." This was the truth.

Julia considered the other woman, frowning. She knew it had been a long shot. Her sigh was heavy as she spoke.

"It was worth a try, anyway." Her smile faltered as she stepped away from the counter. "I guess I can always try her at work on Monday."

"Where are you staying?" Deb knew she shouldn't ask. She even knew that she probably shouldn't get involved. But the look on Julia's face spoke volumes. "Maybe I can call around later on today and see if I can find her."

Julia eyed her, suspecting that Deb knew more than she was willing to tell. But it was another shot worth taking.

"I'm at the Park Plaza downtown. She can find me there."

"I'll let her know." Deb told her, then tried to cover her mistake. "If I find her," she added quickly.

Julia lifted one corner of her mouth in a knowing acknowledgment. "Thank you." She inclined her head. "I appreciate it." She lifted a hand before turning and stepping through the door and out to the waiting taxi.

Deb waited until she saw the cab leave the parking lot. Then she picked up the phone and dialed Cory's phone number.

"Hello?"

"Cory? You sound awful."

"I feel awful." And she did. She hadn't slept well, and her eyes still hurt from the unwelcome tears she had shed.

"Are you okay?"

Cory closed her eyes. She'd already decided that she wasn't going to tell anyone about seeing Jules the day before. Or about the hundred or so women who had passed before her.

"I'm okay. No more. No less."

Deb recognized the sadness in Cory's voice and hoped she was making the right decision.

"Listen, Cory. Someone was just in here looking for you."

"Who was it?"

"Julia Westgate."

Cory sat bolt upright. She tried not to let herself react to the sound of Julia's name. Then she tried to calm her loudly beating heart.

"What did she want?" she asked, trying to sound casual.

"She said that she went by your old apartment and you weren't there. That she's trying to find you."

"What did you tell her?"

"That I would pass along the message if I talked to you. She's staying at the Park Plaza downtown."

Cory was silent. Part of her wanted to run to her car and drive there immediately. But the part that was hurt and humiliated wanted to get in the car and head out of town.

"She also mentioned that if she didn't find you by Monday that she'd try to catch you at work."

Cory groaned silently.

"Thanks, Deb. I really appreciate you letting me know." She closed her eyes, uncertain what to do.

"No problem, Cory," she paused. "But sooner or later, I sure hope you tell me everything that's going on." Her curiosity was more than piqued.

Cory managed a laugh. "I promise, Deb. Thanks again."

They ended the conversation and Cory hung up the phone, paralyzed.

Chapter 20

Julia wasn't quite sure what to do with herself. She had thought by Deb's reaction that she was going to pick up the phone and call Cory the moment she was out the door. So she had gone back to her hotel, hoping that Cory would eventually call.

But after nearly five hours, she had lost all hope. Going stir-crazy, she decided to venture outside and get some fresh air.

It was probably much worse than she'd anticipated. Whatever Raymond had said must have really sent Cory over the edge. There was no doubt that Julia had made too many assumptions. First, that Cory returned her feelings. Second, that she would give her another chance. Last, that Cory would drop everything and come running as soon as she found out that Julia was looking for her.

Then again, maybe Deb hadn't even called her. *Time to move on to plan B.* As she strolled through Copley Square and on to Newbury Street, she decided to look for a newspaper and plot her strategy for Monday.

She found a copy of the *Tribune* and moved on to an outdoor café just a few doors down. She ordered a small cappuccino, and, once settled, began flipping through the newspaper.

She found two pictures from the shoot the day before. The first was of three younger models posed on the rock formation and the other was of Enid Goldman as she observed the scene of photographers and models from afar. The article was brief, with no byline. But Julia assumed that they were Cory's words.

Cory. She put her fingers to the bridge of her nose and closed her eyes. *What was she going to do now?*

She felt something brushing her thigh and, startled, she opened both eyes abruptly. A golden paw brushed her leg.

"Well, look at you," Julia cooed as she stared into a pair of intelligent brown eyes. The dog sat quietly at her side, content.

Curious, Julia lifted a hand, holding it out for the dog's inspection. A tail wagged with approval, and Julia turned to give the animal her full attention. She scratched the dog's head and neck, enjoying the apparent happiness in the brown eyes.

"Who do you belong to, sweetie?" Julia lifted her eyes, looking for the dog's owner. But no one seemed to notice that she had a new friend.

"Is someone missing you?" she asked, growing concerned. She spotted the tags dangling from the dog's collar, and she reached down to get a better look.

Her heart nearly stopped as she read. *Sophie.* Could it be?

"Sophie?" Again she glanced around, spotting no one. "Is it you?" She left her chair and squatted down on the pavement to get closer. "Do you know me, sweetie?"

She turned the nametag over, tears nearly forming as she read Cory's name and address on the back.

Her heart grew warm, and she hugged the dog, enjoying the nose that nuzzled against her neck. "It is you, Sophie. And you're beautiful. And all grown up." She rubbed her ears, enjoying the moment, glancing around yet again.

Then she got to her feet and leaned over. "Where's your mama, Sophie? Is she hiding nearby somewhere?"

She was rewarded with a wag of a tail and a single loud bark. Then Sophie turned and began a slow prance through the tables and around the corner of the restaurant. Cory knelt to receive her greeting.

Julia stopped short of reaching for Cory. Instead she held back, waiting for Cory to stand.

"She's grown quite beautiful," she said quietly, looking for a safe open to conversation. "And it looks like her legs are good and strong."

Cory nodded from where she knelt, afraid to look up into Julia's eyes. She had forgotten the effect that the sound of Julia's voice had on her. Cory's nerves stood on edge, and a jumble of emotions ran through her all at the same time.

"Strong and healthy," she finally said awkwardly. Then she pulled a leash out of her pocket and snapped it onto Sophie's collar. She couldn't put it off any longer, so she gathered her own strength and stood, facing the woman that she hated and loved all at once.

Julia's smile was cautious as she recognized the pinched look on Cory's face. This was going to be quite difficult after all.

"Hullo," she began, searching for something to say. "You look good," she finally added lamely.

Cory's smile was sardonic. "Strong and healthy," she repeated, her words clipped. "You look different."

Julia's hand went to the auburn curls at her neck. "Yes, I suppose I do." She tried to keep her voice light, choosing to ignore the sarcasm in Cory's.

"How did you find me here?" she asked.

"We saw you leaving the hotel. So we followed you." She avoided the violet eyes that threatened to pull her in. The truth was that she and Sophie had sat outside in Copley Square for over an hour while she debated whether or not to set foot in the hotel. When she spotted Julia leaving, her mind had been made up for her.

Julia remained cautious. "I'm glad you found me. Thanks for coming."

Cory shrugged. "I decided it was better this way then to have some kind of a scene down at the paper on Monday."

Julia felt Cory's anger. "I hadn't exactly planned a scene," she said quietly. "I was thinking more along the lines of a reunion."

Cory ignored the comment but couldn't control the guffaw that passed her lips. They were silent while.

"So what did you want? Why were you looking for me?" she finally asked, able to meet Julia's eyes with her own cold ones.

"I wanted to talk with you. To apologize and try to explain everything," she began.

"It's not necessary. I think I understand everything perfectly now."

Julia frowned. "I'm sorry about the fiasco with Raymond yesterday. Believe it or not, long before yesterday I had planned on finding you this weekend. And I had no idea that you would be there."

Cory heard Julia's words, uncertain whether to believe her. Her eyes were daggers as she smiled coldly. "And why should I believe anything you tell me now, *Jules*?" She overemphasized the name that Julia had given her and was almost glad when she saw that Julia cringed.

"I suppose I deserve that. In fact, I know that I do." Jules crossed her arms, feeling a sudden chill. "I don't suppose there's anywhere we could go to sit down and talk?"

"About what?" Cory wanted to hurt her. But Julia was patient.

"About everything that's happened since I saw you last. About what happened when I was here before." She paused, searching for a response on Cory's closed features. "About us."

"There is no *us*, Jules." Her anger flared.

Sophie was growing impatient, and the breeze was becoming cool. Cory let herself glance at Julia, and her resolve began to weaken.

"We can go to my place," she finally said. "I'm

parked a few blocks over." Without waiting for a reply, she and Sophie trotted away, with Julia several steps behind.

They drove in virtual silence, arriving at Cory's home some twenty minutes later.

Julia was pleasantly surprised by Cory's new home, and she took a moment to gaze out at the ocean before wandering inside. She found Cory kneeling in front of the fireplace, building a small fire.

"It's getting chilly," she explained unnecessarily.

"Your home is lovely," Julia replied as she gazed about the living room. "And the view of the ocean is most impressive."

Cory didn't respond. At another time she might have explained how Edgar had given her the place for next to nothing. She would have grabbed Julia's hand and led her about, showing her all of the special nooks and crannies that she had discovered on the property. But it wasn't the same now. And what would be the point?

In spite of herself, Julia grew impatient.

"Cory, please. We need to talk."

"I'm all ears," was Cory's flip reply.

Gritting her teeth, Julia joined her on the floor, carefully keeping her legs several inches from Cory's. She quickly found that she didn't even know where to start.

"Did you know I would be there yesterday?" she finally asked. "Or did you just happen to stumble over me?"

Cory continued to give her full attention to the fire.

"I thought you might be there. So I took the story."

Julia studied her profile. "So you had figured out who I was."

Cory bit back sarcasm. Almost. "I figured it out eventually. I don't usually read fashion magazines, but I saw the interview you did for *Vogue* back in January." She slid a look at the other woman. "I wasn't sure it was you at first. But your eyes are a unique color." She studied them briefly. "Maybe you should consider wearing colored contact lenses for your next weekend fling." She smiled at her own caustic words. But when she got no response from Julia, she turned back to the fire. "Anyway, I figured out that it was you. And once I knew your name, it was easy to find your face all over the Internet."

"But you didn't try to reach me? Even once you knew who I was?" Julia was curious.

Cory was pissed.

"Why would I try to reach you? You knew who *I* was. You could have reached *me* whenever you wanted to." Blood pumping, she began to gather steam. "I had already figured out that you lied to me and played me for a fool that entire weekend. Why would I want to actually hear you say it? Why would I put myself through that kind of humiliation?"

Julia's heart began to ache. "Cory, I am so sorry. But I swear it's not the way you think it is."

"Bullshit." Cory jumped to her feet. "If you were sorry, you would have called me months ago. If you cared at all, you would have told me who you were. You would have let me know it was only for a weekend instead of letting me think it was something more."

Tear of frustration began to pool. "I was such an idiot, Jules. I kept waiting for you to call. Waiting to

141

hear from you. I actually believed that it was the start of something wonderful."

Julia climbed to her feet. "Cory, it *was* the start —" She reached over, touching Cory's arm briefly before Cory pulled away from her.

"Bullshit." Cory screamed the word this time. "You were lying to me every single minute that we were together."

"Cory . . ." Again Julia moved to touch her, but Cory moved beyond her reach.

Tears began to find their way down Cory's cheeks, and she brushed them aside angrily. She didn't want Julia to see her cry. She didn't want her to know how much she cared.

When Julia reached for her again, Cory broke out of her arms and headed straight for the door. The ocean breeze slapped at her cheeks as she found her way down the back steps and onto the lawn. Then she kept walking until she'd reached the rocks and the path that led to the beach below. She stood there, staring out at a calming sea. In that moment, she hated herself for still caring about Julia, and she hated Julia for being the source of so much turmoil in her heart.

But the hatred finally gave way to frustration, then to sadness. She had worked so hard to get past all of this. To let go of ever seeing Julia again. She knew she could get there again. After all, Julia would be leaving again shortly. Maybe the best thing they could do would be to try to work through some of this. Maybe then she could put it behind her and move on.

She felt Julia's presence beside her, and allowed herself to feel the warmth of just knowing she was close by. Collecting her thoughts, she continued to look out at the ocean while she spoke, quietly and in control.

"How many women were there over the years? Have there really been a hundred?" She turned briefly to Julia, making sure that Julia caught the small smile on her lips.

Julia groaned. "Nowhere near," she sighed. "I'm really sorry about Raymond. He can be such a prick when he wants to be."

Cory accepted the apology and waited for Julia to continue.

"There have been closer to a dozen or so," she finally said uncomfortably. "None that I'm particularly proud of."

"And you never told them who you were?"

"Only the first," Julia replied honestly, feeling the shame of what she had done to so many. "And that turned into an utter fiasco. She haunted me, tracked me down. She even threatened to out me in the tabloids."

Cory studied her face. "What happened?"

"Raymond took care of it. I don't know what he did exactly, and I never asked." She was talking out loud, but not really directing her words at Cory. "I was very young then, naive and quite foolish." An image of Carmen flashed in her mind, and she shook her head.

"Things changed quite a bit after that. I became very secretive about my affairs and very protective of my identity." She chanced a look at Cory and found her quietly attentive.

"I'm not making excuses for what I did. But my life really wasn't my own. I had no personal life to speak of, and Raymond had his thumb on my head. I gave him far too much control."

Cory thought that she might understand this. But she couldn't excuse it. "And just how many hearts have you broken, Julia Westgate?" She kept her voice light, trying to tease her without being hurtful.

Julia found a smile, content with the fact that Cory's anger seemed to have dissipated.

"Only Carmen's. The first one," she admitted guiltily. "The truth is, most of the women I had affairs with really only wanted the same thing. I usually made sure of that before I got involved."

Cory's eyes narrowed. "But you didn't with me."

Their eyes met, each woman feeling her own pain.

"No. I didn't with you." Julia's throat hurt. She was tired. And cold. She dug her hands into the pockets of her jacket and tried to ignore the wind that was beginning to whip against her cheeks.

"Cory," the name came out like a sigh. She would do anything to take it all back now. To take away the pain that she found in those eyes. "It's true that my intentions were less than honorable when I met you. But I think I was honest about that, at least the first night."

Cory wanted to deny it and argue the point, but she couldn't. Julia's intentions that night had been quite clear.

"But believe it or not, something happened to me that weekend that had never happened before." She sniffed a little, thinking back to that weekend. A fond smile emerged on her lips as she remembered. "I think it was the moment that I walked down the hallway at the kennel and saw Sophie in your arms. The look on your face nearly made my heart stop."

Julia's smile began to wane. "I started caring about you that very moment, and I didn't know what to do with that. I've never really cared about anyone before. Not like that."

Cory searched her eyes, wanting to believe her.

"And so you just left? Because you cared?" It made no sense.

"No. I left because it was the only thing that I knew how to do. I knew that if I stayed another moment I would tell you everything, and that scared the hell out of me." She shivered as a gust of cold air blew in off the ocean. "Why do you think I couldn't make love with you on that Sunday night? It wasn't because I didn't want to. It was because I knew that I was leaving in a few hours and that it would have made the betrayal all the worse. I couldn't make love with you, feeling the way I did, only to leave you."

Cory's emotions were teetering. She didn't want to hear any of this, and yet she continued to ask questions.

"Why didn't you try to reach me? Why wait until now to track me down?"

Julia's sigh was heavy. "It took me a while to figure out what I was feeling. I couldn't really put a name on it." Her laugh was almost shy. "And once I figured it all out, I knew that a phone call or a letter wouldn't be enough. When I learned about the shoot on the Cape, I focused all of my energy into knowing that I would find you and try to explain once I was here."

Cory felt a small crack in her heart where hope began to take shape. Then she wrapped her arms around herself, the cold finally seeping in. She stared into those violet eyes, seeing the hurt and confusion that she knew too well.

Then her heart sank just as quickly. What was she thinking? In another day or two Julia would be off again.

"What do you want from me, Jules?" An edge had crept back in her voice.

"A chance. I don't expect your forgiveness. I know how much I've hurt you and don't expect that you can understand why I did what I did. But I'm hoping that you'll give me a chance to show you who I really am. I'm hoping that you'll give me more than five minutes to try to explain my entire life."

Cory knew she could melt, but she wouldn't allow herself. "When are you leaving?" She asked abruptly. "How much time are you giving me?" She didn't hide the sarcasm.

Julia blinked hard.

"I'm not going anywhere," she said simply, remembering the freedom that was so recently hers. "Well, except back to my hotel at some point, I suppose. And there are a few things that I still need to take care of back home." She paused, mindful that she was confusing Cory. "Of course there are details that I need to work out. A visa and a green card, and citizenship. Things like that."

Cory's heart was beginning to thud in earnest.

"What are you saying?"

"I've quit the business, Cory." Julia looked away only briefly. "It was only a matter of time, really. But I wanted to leave on my terms, not Raymond's. So I told him. Yesterday. I have nothing else planned. No plane to catch, and nothing that I have to do."

Julia was watching Cory for any reaction. But Cory's expression was carefully blank.

"The only plan I have right now is to be with you. If you'll let me."

"You quit?" Cory asked dumbly.

Julia nodded. "I did. I don't quite know what I'm going to do with myself for the next fifty years, but I figure I have plenty of time to decide."

"You plan on staying here for a while?" Cory didn't believe what she was hearing.

Julia smiled, finally seeing the crack in Cory's composure.

"As long as you'll have me." She raised both brows hopefully and reached out to take Cory's hand. "Please give me another chance, Cory. I know how much I hurt you. But I promise that I'm not going anywhere."

"Jules. You lied to me. I don't know if I can ever trust you."

Julia's lips pulled into a frown. "I know that. All I can tell you is that I promise I'll be honest with you. No matter what."

Cory didn't — couldn't — reply, and so Julia took her other hand cautiously. "Can you find it in your heart to start all over again?"

Cory felt her resolve weakening.

"I still don't believe you," she said, unable to meet Julia's eyes.

"Cory. You may not believe it, but I've never felt anything like this before. In a single weekend my life changed. For nine months I've thought of little else. The only thing that's mattered to me is getting back here to you." A smile touched her lips. "I think I fell in love with you in one short weekend. I can hardly believe it myself, but it's the truth." She stopped only long enough to gauge Cory's reaction. "If I can feel so strongly about you after just one weekend, I can only imagine how I might feel over time. Please give us a chance. Unless you don't feel the same way. If you don't have feelings for me, then you can send me away."

She can't possibly be saying these words to me.

Cory lifted her head, searching Julia's eyes, looking for the lies that she thought must certainly be there. But Julia's eyes were open, honest, and sincere.

Cory tried to hold back her hopeful heart but failed.

"You already know that I fell in love with you."

For the first time in months, Julia felt her heart begin to soar.

"You did? Really?"

They could both hear barking from a distance, and they turned to see Sophie pawing at the screen door.

"I did. Really. As much as it pains me to admit it." Cory was grimacing, but her heart wasn't in it. "And don't try to tell me that you didn't know."

Sophie's bark was becoming insistent, nearly distracting them both.

"Can you ever forgive me?" Julia's voice was earnest.

"I don't know, Jules," she sighed. "But I want to try."

Ecstatic, Julia covered the small space between them and gathered Cory up in her arms. They held each other for the longest time, each reveling in the feel of the other's nearness.

"I can't tell you how many times I've thought about holding you like this," Julia whispered against her ear.

Cory felt nervous laughter bubbling. She could still hear Sophie barking.

"I am so mad at you." She lifted her head, shocked to find herself staring into the most beautiful eyes she'd ever seen. Then she was leaning forward and planting a deep, hard kiss on Julia's mouth.

"I'll make it up to you," Julia beamed. "I promise."

Then Sophie was upon them, jumping up and nearly toppling them both. They broke apart only long enough to regain their balance and give Sophie a moment of their attention. Then they were in each other's arms again, neither willing to let go.

LOOKING FOR NAIAD?

Buy our books at
www.naiadpress.com

or call our toll-free number
1-800-533-1973

or by fax (24 hours a day)
1-850-539-9731

A few of the publications of
THE NAIAD PRESS, INC.
P.O. Box 10543   Tallahassee, Florida 32302
Phone (850) 539-5965
Toll-Free Order Number: 1-800-533-1973
Web Site: WWW.NAIADPRESS.COM
Mail orders welcome. Please include 15% postage.
Write or call for our free catalog which also features an
incredible selection of lesbian videos.

CHANGE OF HEART by Linda Hill. 176 pp. High fashion and
love in a glamorous world.   ISBN 1-56280-238-0 $11.95

UNSTRUNG HEART by Robbi Sommers. 176 pp. Putting life
in order again.   ISBN 1-56280-239-9   11.95

BIRDS OF A FEATHER by Jackie Calhoun. 240 pp. Life begins
with love.   ISBN 1-56280-240-2   11.95

THE DRIVE by Trisha Todd. 176 pp. The star of *Claire of the
Moon* tells all!   ISBN 1-56280-237-2   11.95

BOTH SIDES by Saxon Bennett. 240 pp. A community of
women falling in and out of love.   ISBN 1-56280-236-4   11.95

WATERMARK by Karin Kallmaker. 256 pp. One burning
question . . . how to lead her back to love? ISBN 1-56280-235-6   11.95

THE OTHER WOMAN by Ann O'Leary. 240 pp. Her roguish
way draws women like a magnet.   ISBN 1-56280-234-8   11.95

SILVER THREADS by Lyn Denison.208 pp. Finding her way
back to love . . .   ISBN 1-56280-231-3   11.95

CHIMNEY ROCK BLUES by Janet McClellan. 224 pp. 4th Tru
North mystery.   ISBN 1-56280-233-X   11.95

OMAHA'S BELL by Penny Hayes. 208 pp. Orphaned Keeley
Delaney woos the lovely Prudence Morris. ISBN 1-56280-232-1   11.95

SIXTH SENSE by Kate Calloway. 224 pp. 6th Cassidy James
mystery.   ISBN 1-56280-228-3   11.95

DAWN OF THE DANCE by Marianne K. Martin. 224 pp. A dance
with an old friend, nothing more . . . yeah! ISBN 1-56280-229-1   11.95

WEDDING BELL BLUES by Julia Watts. 240 pp. Love, family,
and a recipe for success.   ISBN 1-56280-230-5   11.95

THOSE WHO WAIT by Peggy J. Herring. 160 pp. Two
sisters . . . in love with the same woman. ISBN 1-56280-223-2   11.95

WHISPERS IN THE WIND by Frankie J. Jones. 192 pp. "If you
don't want this," she whispered, "all you have to say is 'stop.' "
ISBN 1-56280-226-7   11.95

WHEN SOME BODY DISAPPEARS by Therese Szymanski.
192 pp. 3rd Brett Higgins mystery.   ISBN 1-56280-227-5   11.95

THE WAY LIFE SHOULD BE by Diana Braund. 240 pp. Which
one will teach her the true meaning of love?   ISBN 1-56280-221-6   11.95

UNTIL THE END by Kaye Davis. 256pp. 3rd Maris Middleton
mystery.   ISBN 1-56280-222-4   11.95

FIFTH WHEEL by Kate Calloway. 224 pp. 5th Cassidy James
mystery.   ISBN 1-56280-218-6   11.95

JUST YESTERDAY by Linda Hill. 176 pp. Reliving all the
passion of yesterday.   ISBN 1-56280-219-4   11.95

THE TOUCH OF YOUR HAND edited by Barbara Grier and
Christine Cassidy. 304 pp. Erotic love stories by Naiad Press
authors.   ISBN 1-56280-220-8   14.95

WINDROW GARDEN by Janet McClellan. 192 pp. They discover
a passion they never dreamed possible.   ISBN 1-56280-216-X   11.95

PAST DUE by Claire McNab. 224 pp. 10th Carol Ashton
mystery.   ISBN 1-56280-217-8   11.95

CHRISTABEL by Laura Adams. 224 pp. Two captive hearts and
the passion that will set them free.   ISBN 1-56280-214-3   11.95

PRIVATE PASSIONS by Laura DeHart Young. 192 pp. An
unforgettable new portrait of lesbian love . . .   ISBN 1-56280-215-1   11.95

BAD MOON RISING by Barbara Johnson. 208 pp. 2nd Colleen
Fitzgerald mystery.   ISBN 1-56280-211-9   11.95

RIVER QUAY by Janet McClellan. 208 pp. 3rd Tru North
mystery.   ISBN 1-56280-212-7   11.95

ENDLESS LOVE by Lisa Shapiro. 272 pp. To believe, once
again, that love can be forever.   ISBN 1-56280-213-5   11.95

FALLEN FROM GRACE by Pat Welch. 256 pp. 6th Helen Black
mystery.   ISBN 1-56280-209-7   11.95

THE NAKED EYE by Catherine Ennis. 208 pp. Her lover in the
camera's eye . . .   ISBN 1-56280-210-0   11.95

OVER THE LINE by Tracey Richardson. 176 pp. 2nd Stevie
Houston mystery.   ISBN 1-56280-202-X   11.95

JULIA'S SONG by Ann O'Leary. 208 pp. Strangely
disturbing . . . strangely exciting.   ISBN 1-56280-197-X   11.95

LOVE IN THE BALANCE by Marianne K. Martin. 256 pp.
Weighing the costs of love . . .   ISBN 1-56280-199-6   11.95

PIECE OF MY HEART by Julia Watts. 208 pp. All the
stuff that dreams are made of —   ISBN 1-56280-206-2   11.95

MAKING UP FOR LOST TIME by Karin Kallmaker. 240 pp.
Nobody does it better . . .   ISBN 1-56280-196-1   11.95

GOLD FEVER by Lyn Denison. 224 pp. By author of *Dream Lover.*   ISBN 1-56280-201-1   11.95

WHEN THE DEAD SPEAK by Therese Szymanski. 224 pp. 2nd
Brett Higgins mystery.   ISBN 1-56280-198-8   11.95

FOURTH DOWN by Kate Calloway. 240 pp. 4th Cassidy James
mystery.   ISBN 1-56280-205-4   11.95

A MOMENT'S INDISCRETION by Peggy J. Herring. 176 pp.
There's a fine line between love and lust . . .   ISBN 1-56280-194-5   11.95

CITY LIGHTS/COUNTRY CANDLES by Penny Hayes. 208 pp.
About the women she has known . . .   ISBN 1-56280-195-3   11.95

POSSESSIONS by Kaye Davis. 240 pp. 2nd Maris Middleton
mystery.   ISBN 1-56280-192-9   11.95

A QUESTION OF LOVE by Saxon Bennett. 208 pp. Every
woman is granted one great love.   ISBN 1-56280-205-4   11.95

RHYTHM TIDE by Frankie J. Jones. 160 pp. . . . to desire
passionately and be passionately desired.   ISBN 1-56280-189-9   11.95

PENN VALLEY PHOENIX by Janet McClellan. 208 pp. 2nd
Tru North Mystery.   ISBN 1-56280-200-3   11.95

BY RESERVATION ONLY by Jackie Calhoun. 240 pp. A
chance for true happiness.   ISBN 1-56280-191-0   11.95

OLD BLACK MAGIC by Jaye Maiman. 272 pp. 9th Robin
Miller mystery.   ISBN 1-56280-175-9   11.95

LEGACY OF LOVE by Marianne K. Martin. 240 pp. Women
will do anything for her . . .   ISBN 1-56280-184-8   11.95

LETTING GO by Ann O'Leary. 160 pp. Laura, at 39, in love
with 23-year-old Kate.   ISBN 1-56280-183-X   11.95

LADY BE GOOD edited by Barbara Grier and Christine Cassidy.
288 pp. Erotic stories by Naiad Press authors. ISBN 1-56280-180-5   14.95

CHAIN LETTER by Claire McNab. 288 pp. 9th Carol Ashton
mystery.   ISBN 1-56280-181-3   11.95

NIGHT VISION by Laura Adams. 256 pp. Erotic fantasy romance
by "famous" author.   ISBN 1-56280-182-1   11.95

SEA TO SHINING SEA by Lisa Shapiro. 256 pp. Unable to resist
the raging passion . . .   ISBN 1-56280-177-5   11.95

THIRD DEGREE by Kate Calloway. 224 pp. 3rd Cassidy James
mystery.   ISBN 1-56280-185-6   11.95

WHEN THE DANCING STOPS by Therese Szymanski. 272 pp.
1st Brett Higgins mystery.   ISBN 1-56280-186-4   11.95

PHASES OF THE MOON by Julia Watts. 192 pp. . . . . hungry
for everything life has to offer.   ISBN 1-56280-176-7   11.95

BABY IT'S COLD by Jaye Maiman. 256 pp. 5th Robin Miller
mystery.   ISBN 1-56280-156-2   10.95

CLASS REUNION by Linda Hill. 176 pp. The girl from her
past . . .   ISBN 1-56280-178-3   11.95

DREAM LOVER by Lyn Denison. 224 pp. A soft, sensuous,
romantic fantasy.   ISBN 1-56280-173-1   11.95

FORTY LOVE by Diana Simmonds. 288 pp. Joyous, heart-
warming romance.   ISBN 1-56280-171-6   11.95

IN THE MOOD by Robbi Sommers. 160 pp. The queen of
erotic tension!   ISBN 1-56280-172-4   11.95

SWIMMING CAT COVE by Lauren Douglas. 192 pp. 2nd
Allison O'Neil Mystery.   ISBN 1-56280-168-6   11.95

THE LOVING LESBIAN by Claire McNab and Sharon Gedan.
240 pp. Explore the experiences that make lesbian love unique.
         ISBN 1-56280-169-4   14.95

COURTED by Celia Cohen. 160 pp. Sparkling romantic
encounter.   ISBN 1-56280-166-X   11.95

SEASONS OF THE HEART by Jackie Calhoun. 240 pp. Romance
through the years.   ISBN 1-56280-167-8   11.95

K. C. BOMBER by Janet McClellan. 208 pp. 1st Tru North
mystery.   ISBN 1-56280-157-0   11.95

LAST RITES by Tracey Richardson. 192 pp. 1st Stevie Houston
mystery.   ISBN 1-56280-164-3   11.95

EMBRACE IN MOTION by Karin Kallmaker. 256 pp. A whirlwind
love affair.   ISBN 1-56280-165-1   11.95

HOT CHECK by Peggy J. Herring. 192 pp. Will workaholic Alice
fall for guitarist Ricky?   ISBN 1-56280-163-5   11.95

OLD TIES by Saxon Bennett. 176 pp. Can Cleo surrender to a
passionate new love?   ISBN 1-56280-159-7   11.95

LOVE ON THE LINE by Laura DeHart Young. 176 pp. Will Stef
win Kay's heart?   ISBN 1-56280-162-7   11.95

DEVIL'S LEG CROSSING by Kaye Davis. 192 pp. 1st Maris
Middleton mystery.   ISBN 1-56280-158-9   11.95

COSTA BRAVA by Marta Balletbo Coll. 144 pp. Read the book,
see the movie!   ISBN 1-56280-153-8   11.95

MEETING MAGDALENE & OTHER STORIES by
Marilyn Freeman. 144 pp. Read the book, see the movie!
         ISBN 1-56280-170-8   11.95

SECOND FIDDLE by Kate 208 pp. 2nd P.I. Cassidy James
mystery.   ISBN 1-56280-169-6   11.95

LAUREL by Isabel Miller. 128 pp. By the author of the beloved
Patience and Sarah.   ISBN 1-56280-146-5   10.95

LOVE OR MONEY by Jackie Calhoun. 240 pp. The romance of
real life.   ISBN 1-56280-147-3   10.95

SMOKE AND MIRRORS by Pat Welch. 224 pp. 5th Helen Black
Mystery.   ISBN 1-56280-143-0   10.95

DANCING IN THE DARK edited by Barbara Grier & Christine
Cassidy. 272 pp. Erotic love stories by Naiad Press authors.
                                                ISBN 1-56280-144-9   14.95

TIME AND TIME AGAIN by Catherine Ennis. 176 pp. Passionate
love affair.   ISBN 1-56280-145-7   10.95

PAXTON COURT by Diane Salvatore. 256 pp. Erotic and wickedly
funny contemporary tale about the business of learning to live
together.   ISBN 1-56280-114-7   10.95

INNER CIRCLE by Claire McNab. 208 pp. 8th Carol Ashton
Mystery.   ISBN 1-56280-135-X   11.95

LESBIAN SEX: AN ORAL HISTORY by Susan Johnson.
240 pp. Need we say more?   ISBN 1-56280-142-2   14.95

WILD THINGS by Karin Kallmaker. 240 pp. By the undisputed
mistress of lesbian romance.   ISBN 1-56280-139-2   11.95

THE GIRL NEXT DOOR by Mindy Kaplan. 208 pp. Just what
you d expect.   ISBN 1-56280-140-6   11.95

NOW AND THEN by Penny Hayes. 240 pp. Romance on the
westward journey.   ISBN 1-56280-121-X   11.95

HEART ON FIRE by Diana Simmonds. 176 pp. The romantic and
erotic rival of *Curious Wine*.   ISBN 1-56280-152-X   11.95

DEATH AT LAVENDER BAY by Lauren Wright Douglas. 208 pp.
1st Allison O'Neil Mystery.   ISBN 1-56280-085-X   11.95

YES I SAID YES I WILL by Judith McDaniel. 272 pp. Hot
romance by famous author.   ISBN 1-56280-138-4   11.95

FORBIDDEN FIRES by Margaret C. Anderson. Edited by Mathilda
Hills. 176 pp. Famous author's "unpublished" Lesbian romance.
                                                ISBN 1-56280-123-6   21.95

SIDE TRACKS by Teresa Stores. 160 pp. Gender-bending
Lesbians on the road.   ISBN 1-56280-122-8   10.95

WILDWOOD FLOWERS by Julia Watts. 208 pp. Hilarious and
heart-warming tale of true love.   ISBN 1-56280-127-9   10.95

NEVER SAY NEVER by Linda Hill. 224 pp. Rule #1: Never get
involved with . . .   ISBN 1-56280-126-0   11.95

THE WISH LIST by Saxon Bennett. 192 pp. Romance through
the years.   ISBN 1-56280-125-2   10.95

OUT OF THE NIGHT by Kris Bruyer. 192 pp. Spine-tingling
thriller.   ISBN 1-56280-120-1   10.95

LOVE'S HARVEST by Peggy J. Herring. 176 pp. by the author of
Once More With Feeling.   ISBN 1-56280-117-1   10.95

FAMILY SECRETS by Laura DeHart Young. 208 pp. Enthralling
romance and suspense.   ISBN 1-56280-119-8   10.95

INLAND PASSAGE by Jane Rule. 288 pp. Tales exploring conven-
tional & unconventional relationships.   ISBN 0-930044-56-8   10.95

DOUBLE BLUFF by Claire McNab. 208 pp. 7th Carol Ashton
Mystery.   ISBN 1-56280-096-5   10.95

BAR GIRLS by Lauran Hoffman. 176 pp. See the movie, read
the book!   ISBN 1-56280-115-5   10.95

THE FIRST TIME EVER edited by Barbara Grier & Christine
Cassidy. 272 pp. Love stories by Naiad Press authors.
                                             ISBN 1-56280-086-8   14.95

MISS PETTIBONE AND MISS McGRAW by Brenda Weathers.
208 pp. A charming ghostly love story.   ISBN 1-56280-151-1   10.95

CHANGES by Jackie Calhoun. 208 pp. Involved romance and
relationships.   ISBN 1-56280-083-3   10.95

FAIR PLAY by Rose Beecham. 256 pp. An Amanda Valentine
Mystery.   ISBN 1-56280-081-7   10.95

PAYBACK by Celia Cohen. 176 pp. A gripping thriller of romance,
revenge and betrayal.   ISBN 1-56280-084-1   10.95

THE BEACH AFFAIR by Barbara Johnson. 224 pp. Sizzling
summer romance/mystery/intrigue.   ISBN 1-56280-090-6   10.95

GETTING THERE by Robbi Sommers. 192 pp. Nobody does it
like Robbi!   ISBN 1-56280-099-X   10.95

FINAL CUT by Lisa Haddock. 208 pp. 2nd Carmen Ramirez
Mystery.   ISBN 1-56280-088-4   10.95

FLASHPOINT by Katherine V. Forrest. 256 pp. A Lesbian
blockbuster!   ISBN 1-56280-079-5   10.95

CLAIRE OF THE MOON by Nicole Conn. Audio Book —
Read by Marianne Hyatt.   ISBN 1-56280-113-9   16.95

FOR LOVE AND FOR LIFE: INTIMATE PORTRAITS OF
LESBIAN COUPLES by Susan Johnson. 224 pp.
                                             ISBN 1-56280-091-4   14.95

DEVOTION by Mindy Kaplan. 192 pp. See the movie — read
the book!   ISBN 1-56280-093-0   10.95

SOMEONE TO WATCH by Jaye Maiman. 272 pp. 4th Robin
Miller Mystery.   ISBN 1-56280-095-7   10.95

GREENER THAN GRASS by Jennifer Fulton. 208 pp. A young
woman — a stranger in her bed.   ISBN 1-56280-092-2   10.95

TRAVELS WITH DIANA HUNTER by Regine Sands. Erotic
lesbian romp. Audio Book (2 cassettes)   ISBN 1-56280-107-4   16.95

CABIN FEVER by Carol Schmidt. 256 pp. Sizzling suspense
and passion.   ISBN 1-56280-089-1   10.95

THERE WILL BE NO GOODBYES by Laura DeHart Young. 192
pp. Romantic love, strength, and friendship.   ISBN 1-56280-103-1   10.95

FAULTLINE by Sheila Ortiz Taylor. 144 pp. Joyous comic
lesbian novel.   ISBN 1-56280-108-2   9.95

OPEN HOUSE by Pat Welch. 176 pp. 4th Helen Black Mystery.
                                            ISBN 1-56280-102-3   10.95

ONCE MORE WITH FEELING by Peggy J. Herring. 240 pp.
Lighthearted, loving romantic adventure.   ISBN 1-56280-089-2   11.95

WHISPERS by Kris Bruyer. 176 pp. Romantic ghost story.
                                            ISBN 1-56280-082-5   10.95

NIGHT SONGS by Penny Mickelbury. 224 pp. 2nd Gianna
Maglione Mystery.   ISBN 1-56280-097-3   10.95

GETTING TO THE POINT by Teresa Stores. 256 pp. Classic
southern Lesbian novel.   ISBN 1-56280-100-7   10.95

PAINTED MOON by Karin Kallmaker. 224 pp. Delicious
Kallmaker romance.   ISBN 1-56280-075-2   11.95

THE MYSTERIOUS NAIAD edited by Katherine V. Forrest &
Barbara Grier. 320 pp. Love stories by Naiad Press authors.
                                            ISBN 1-56280-074-4   14.95

DAUGHTERS OF A CORAL DAWN by Katherine V. Forrest.
240 pp. Tenth Anniversay Edition.   ISBN 1-56280-104-X   11.95

BODY GUARD by Claire McNab. 208 pp. 6th Carol Ashton
Mystery.   ISBN 1-56280-073-6   11.95

CACTUS LOVE by Lee Lynch. 192 pp. Stories by the beloved
storyteller.   ISBN 1-56280-071-X   9.95

SECOND GUESS by Rose Beecham. 216 pp. An Amanda
Valentine Mystery.   ISBN 1-56280-069-8   9.95

A RAGE OF MAIDENS by Lauren Wright Douglas. 240 pp.
6th Caitlin Reece Mystery.   ISBN 1-56280-068-X   10.95

TRIPLE EXPOSURE by Jackie Calhoun. 224 pp. Romantic
drama involving many characters.   ISBN 1-56280-067-1   10.95

PERSONAL ADS by Robbi Sommers. 176 pp. Sizzling short
stories.   ISBN 1-56280-059-0   11.95

CROSSWORDS by Penny Sumner. 256 pp. 2nd Victoria Cross
Mystery.   ISBN 1-56280-064-7   9.95

SWEET CHERRY WINE by Carol Schmidt. 224 pp. A novel of
suspense.   ISBN 1-56280-063-9   9.95

CERTAIN SMILES by Dorothy Tell. 160 pp. Erotic short stories.
                                            ISBN 1-56280-066-3   9.95

EDITED OUT by Lisa Haddock. 224 pp. 1st Carmen Ramirez
Mystery.   ISBN 1-56280-077-9   9.95

SMOKEY O by Celia Cohen. 176 pp. Relationships on the
playing field.   ISBN 1-56280-057-4   9.95

KATHLEEN O'DONALD by Penny Hayes. 256 pp. Rose and
Kathleen find each other and employment in 1909 NYC.
                                            ISBN 1-56280-070-1   9.95

STAYING HOME by Elisabeth Nonas. 256 pp. Molly and Alix
want a baby . . . or do they?   ISBN 1-56280-076-0   10.95

TRUE LOVE by Jennifer Fulton. 240 pp. Six lesbians searching
for love in all the "right" places.   ISBN 1-56280-035-3   11.95

KEEPING SECRETS by Penny Mickelbury. 208 pp. 1st Gianna
Maglione Mystery.   ISBN 1-56280-052-3   9.95

THE ROMANTIC NAIAD edited by Katherine V. Forrest &
Barbara Grier. 336 pp. Love stories by Naiad Press authors.
                                            ISBN 1-56280-054-X   14.95

UNDER MY SKIN by Jaye Maiman. 336 pp. 3rd Robin Miller
Mystery.   ISBN 1-56280-049-3.   11.95

CAR POOL by Karin Kallmaker. 272pp. Lesbians on wheels
and then some!   ISBN 1-56280-048-5   11.95

NOT TELLING MOTHER: STORIES FROM A LIFE by Diane
Salvatore. 176 pp. Her 3rd novel.   ISBN 1-56280-044-2   9.95

GOBLIN MARKET by Lauren Wright Douglas. 240pp. 5th Caitlin
Reece Mystery.   ISBN 1-56280-047-7   10.95

FRIENDS AND LOVERS by Jackie Calhoun. 224 pp. Mid-
western Lesbian lives and loves.   ISBN 1-56280-041-8   11.95

BEHIND CLOSED DOORS by Robbi Sommers. 192 pp. Hot,
erotic short stories.   ISBN 1-56280-039-6   11.95

CLAIRE OF THE MOON by Nicole Conn. 192 pp. See the
movie — read the book!   ISBN 1-56280-038-8   11.95

SILENT HEART by Claire McNab. 192 pp. Exotic Lesbian
romance.   ISBN 1-56280-036-1   11.95

THE SPY IN QUESTION by Amanda Kyle Williams. 256 pp.
A Madison McGuire Mystery.   ISBN 1-56280-037-X   9.95

SAVING GRACE by Jennifer Fulton. 240 pp. Adventure and
romantic entanglement.   ISBN 1-56280-051-5   11.95

CURIOUS WINE by Katherine V. Forrest. 176 pp. Tenth Anniver-
sary Edition. The most popular contemporary Lesbian love story.
                                            ISBN 1-56280-053-1   11.95
    Audio Book (2 cassettes)   ISBN 1-56280-105-8   16.95

CHAUTAUQUA by Catherine Ennis. 192 pp. Exciting, romantic
adventure.   ISBN 1-56280-032-9   9.95

A PROPER BURIAL by Pat Welch. 192 pp. 3rd Helen Black
Mystery.   ISBN 1-56280-033-7   9.95

SILVERLAKE HEAT: A Novel of Suspense by Carol Schmidt.
240 pp. Rhonda is as hot as Laney's dreams.   ISBN 1-56280-031-0   9.95

LOVE, ZENA BETH by Diane Salvatore. 224 pp. The most talked
about lesbian novel of the nineties!   ISBN 1-56280-030-2   10.95

A DOORYARD FULL OF FLOWERS by Isabel Miller. 160 pp.
Stories incl. 2 sequels to *Patience and Sarah.*   ISBN 1-56280-029-9   9.95

MURDER BY TRADITION by Katherine V. Forrest. 288 pp. 4th
Kate Delafield Mystery.   ISBN 1-56280-002-7   11.95

THE EROTIC NAIAD edited by Katherine V. Forrest & Barbara
Grier. 224 pp. Love stories by Naiad Press authors.
                                             ISBN 1-56280-026-4   14.95

DEAD CERTAIN by Claire McNab. 224 pp. 5th Carol Ashton
Mystery.   ISBN 1-56280-027-2   9.95

CRAZY FOR LOVING by Jaye Maiman. 320 pp. 2nd Robin Miller
Mystery.   ISBN 1-56280-025-6   11.95

UNCERTAIN COMPANIONS by Robbi Sommers. 204 pp.
Steamy, erotic novel.   ISBN 1-56280-017-5   11.95

A TIGER'S HEART by Lauren W. Douglas. 240 pp. 4th Caitlin
Reece Mystery.   ISBN 1-56280-018-3   9.95

PAPERBACK ROMANCE by Karin Kallmaker. 256 pp. A
delicious romance.   ISBN 1-56280-019-1   10.95

THE LAVENDER HOUSE MURDER by Nikki Baker. 224 pp.
2nd Virginia Kelly Mystery.   ISBN 1-56280-012-4   9.95

PASSION BAY by Jennifer Fulton. 224 pp. Passionate romance,
virgin beaches, tropical skies.   ISBN 1-56280-028-0   10.95

STICKS AND STONES by Jackie Calhoun. 208 pp. Contemporary
lesbian lives and loves.   ISBN 1-56280-020-5   9.95
Audio Book (2 cassettes)   ISBN 1-56280-106-6   16.95

UNDER THE SOUTHERN CROSS by Claire McNab. 192 pp.
Romantic nights Down Under.   ISBN 1-56280-011-6   11.95

GRASSY FLATS by Penny Hayes. 256 pp. Lesbian romance in
the '30s.   ISBN 1-56280-010-8   9.95

THE END OF APRIL by Penny Sumner. 240 pp. 1st Victoria
Cross Mystery.   ISBN 1-56280-007-8   8.95

KISS AND TELL by Robbi Sommers. 192 pp. Scorching stories
by the author of *Pleasures.*   ISBN 1-56280-005-1   11.95

STILL WATERS by Pat Welch. 208 pp. 2nd Helen Black Mystery.
                                             ISBN 0-941483-97-5   9.95

TO LOVE AGAIN by Evelyn Kennedy. 208 pp. Wildly romantic
love story.   ISBN 0-941483-85-1   11.95

IN THE GAME by Nikki Baker. 192 pp. 1st Virginia Kelly
Mystery.   ISBN 1-56280-004-3   9.95

STRANDED by Camarin Grae. 320 pp. Entertaining, riveting
adventure.   ISBN 0-941483-99-1   9.95

THE DAUGHTERS OF ARTEMIS by Lauren Wright Douglas.
240 pp. 3rd Caitlin Reece Mystery.   ISBN 0-941483-95-9   9.95

CLEARWATER by Catherine Ennis. 176 pp. Romantic secrets
of a small Louisiana town.   ISBN 0-941483-65-7   8.95

THE HALLELUJAH MURDERS by Dorothy Tell. 176 pp. 2nd
Poppy Dillworth Mystery.   ISBN 0-941483-88-6   8.95

BENEDICTION by Diane Salvatore. 272 pp. Striking, contemporary romantic novel.   ISBN 0-941483-90-8   11.95

COP OUT by Claire McNab. 208 pp. 4th Carol Ashton Mystery.
                                      ISBN 0-941483-84-3   10.95

THE BEVERLY MALIBU by Katherine V. Forrest. 288 pp. 3rd
Kate Delafield Mystery.   ISBN 0-941483-48-7   11.95

THE PROVIDENCE FILE by Amanda Kyle Williams. 256 pp.
A Madison McGuire Mystery.   ISBN 0-941483-92-4   8.95

I LEFT MY HEART by Jaye Maiman. 320 pp. 1st Robin Miller
Mystery.   ISBN 0-941483-72-X   11.95

THE PRICE OF SALT by Patricia Highsmith (writing as Claire
Morgan). 288 pp. Classic lesbian novel, first issued in 1952 . . .
acknowledged by its author under her own, very famous, name.
                                      ISBN 1-56280-003-5   11.95

SIDE BY SIDE by Isabel Miller. 256 pp. From beloved author of
Patience and Sarah.   ISBN 0-941483-77-0   10.95

STAYING POWER: LONG TERM LESBIAN COUPLES by
Susan E. Johnson. 352 pp. Joys of coupledom. ISBN 0-941-483-75-4 14.95

SLICK by Camarin Grae. 304 pp. Exotic, erotic adventure.
                                      ISBN 0-941483-74-6   9.95

NINTH LIFE by Lauren Wright Douglas. 256 pp. 2nd Caitlin
Reece Mystery.   ISBN 0-941483-50-9   9.95

PLAYERS by Robbi Sommers. 192 pp. Sizzling, erotic novel.
                                      ISBN 0-941483-73-8   9.95

MURDER AT RED ROOK RANCH by Dorothy Tell. 224 pp.
1st Poppy Dillworth Mystery.   ISBN 0-941483-80-0   8.95

A ROOM FULL OF WOMEN by Elisabeth Nonas. 256 pp.
Contemporary Lesbian lives.   ISBN 0-941483-69-X   9.95

THEME FOR DIVERSE INSTRUMENTS by Jane Rule. 208 pp.
Powerful romantic lesbian stories.   ISBN 0-941483-63-0   8.95

CLUB 12 by Amanda Kyle Williams. 288 pp. Espionage thriller
featuring a lesbian agent!   ISBN 0-941483-64-9   9.95

DEATH DOWN UNDER by Claire McNab. 240 pp. 3rd Carol
Ashton Mystery.   ISBN 0-941483-39-8   11.95

MONTANA FEATHERS by Penny Hayes. 256 pp. Vivian and
Elizabeth find love in frontier Montana.   ISBN 0-941483-61-4   9.95

THERE'S SOMETHING I'VE BEEN MEANING TO TELL YOU
Ed. by Loralee MacPike. 288 pp. Gay men and lesbians coming out
to their children.   ISBN 0-941483-44-4   9.95

LIFTING BELLY by Gertrude Stein. Ed. by Rebecca Mark. 104 pp.
Erotic poetry.   ISBN 0-941483-51-7   10.95

AFTER THE FIRE by Jane Rule. 256 pp. Warm, human novel by
this incomparable author.   ISBN 0-941483-45-2   8.95

PLEASURES by Robbi Sommers. 204 pp. Unprecedented
eroticism.   ISBN 0-941483-49-5   11.95

EDGEWISE by Camarin Grae. 372 pp. Spellbinding
adventure.   ISBN 0-941483-19-3   9.95

FATAL REUNION by Claire McNab. 224 pp. 2nd Carol Ashton
Mystery.   ISBN 0-941483-40-1   11.95

IN EVERY PORT by Karin Kallmaker. 228 pp. Jessica's sexy,
adventuresome travels.   ISBN 0-941483-37-7   11.95

OF LOVE AND GLORY by Evelyn Kennedy. 192 pp. Exciting
WWII romance.   ISBN 0-941483-32-0   10.95

CLICKING STONES by Nancy Tyler Glenn. 288 pp. Love
transcending time.   ISBN 0-941483-31-2   9.95

SOUTH OF THE LINE by Catherine Ennis. 216 pp. Civil War
adventure.   ISBN 0-941483-29-0   8.95

WOMAN PLUS WOMAN by Dolores Klaich. 300 pp. Supurb
Lesbian overview.   ISBN 0-941483-28-2   9.95

THE FINER GRAIN by Denise Ohio. 216 pp. Brilliant young
college lesbian novel.   ISBN 0-941483-11-8   8.95

LESSONS IN MURDER by Claire McNab. 216 pp. 1st Carol Ashton
Mystery.   ISBN 0-941483-14-2   11.95

YELLOWTHROAT by Penny Hayes. 240 pp. Margarita, bandit,
kidnaps Julia.   ISBN 0-941483-10-X   8.95

SAPPHISTRY: THE BOOK OF LESBIAN SEXUALITY by
Pat Califia. 3d edition, revised. 208 pp.   ISBN 0-941483-24-X   12.95

CHERISHED LOVE by Evelyn Kennedy. 192 pp. Erotic Lesbian
love story.   ISBN 0-941483-08-8   11.95

THE SECRET IN THE BIRD by Camarin Grae. 312 pp. Striking,
psychological suspense novel.   ISBN 0-941483-05-3   8.95

TO THE LIGHTNING by Catherine Ennis. 208 pp. Romantic
Lesbian `Robinson Crusoe adventure.   ISBN 0-941483-06-1   8.95

DREAMS AND SWORDS by Katherine V. Forrest. 192 pp.
Romantic, erotic, imaginative stories.　　ISBN 0-941483-03-7　　11.95

MEMORY BOARD by Jane Rule. 336 pp. Memorable novel
about an aging Lesbian couple.　　ISBN 0-941483-02-9　　12.95

THE ALWAYS ANONYMOUS BEAST by Lauren Wright Douglas.
224 pp. 1st Caitlin Reece Mystery.　　ISBN 0-941483-04-5　　8.95

MURDER AT THE NIGHTWOOD BAR by Katherine V. Forrest.
240 pp. 2nd Kate Delafield Mystery.　　ISBN 0-930044-92-4　　11.95

WINGED DANCER by Camarin Grae. 228 pp. Erotic Lesbian
adventure story.　　ISBN 0-930044-88-6　　8.95

PAZ by Camarin Grae. 336 pp. Romantic Lesbian adventurer
with the power to change the world.　　ISBN 0-930044-89-4　　8.95

SOUL SNATCHER by Camarin Grae. 224 pp. A puzzle, an
adventure, a mystery — Lesbian romance.　　ISBN 0-930044-90-8　　8.95

THE LOVE OF GOOD WOMEN by Isabel Miller. 224 pp.
Long-awaited new novel by the author of the beloved *Patience
and Sarah*.　　ISBN 0-930044-81-9　　8.95

THE LONG TRAIL by Penny Hayes. 248 pp. Vivid adventures
of two women in love in the old west.　　ISBN 0-930044-76-2　　8.95

AN EMERGENCE OF GREEN by Katherine V. Forrest. 288
pp. Powerful novel of sexual discovery.　　ISBN 0-930044-69-X　　11.95

DESERT OF THE HEART by Jane Rule. 224 pp. A classic;
basis for the movie *Desert Hearts*.　　ISBN 0-930044-73-8　　11.95

SEX VARIANT WOMEN IN LITERATURE by Jeannette
Howard Foster. 448 pp. Literary history.　　ISBN 0-930044-65-7　　8.95

A HOT-EYED MODERATE by Jane Rule. 252 pp. Hard-hitting
essays on gay life; writing; art.　　ISBN 0-930044-57-6　　7.95

AMATEUR CITY by Katherine V. Forrest. 224 pp. 1st Kate
Delafield Mystery.　　ISBN 0-930044-55-X　　10.95

THE SOPHIE HOROWITZ STORY by Sarah Schulman. 176 pp.
Engaging novel of madcap intrigue.　　ISBN 0-930044-54-1　　7.95

THE YOUNG IN ONE ANOTHER'S ARMS by Jane Rule.
224 pp. Classic Jane Rule.　　ISBN 0-930044-53-3　　9.95

AGAINST THE SEASON by Jane Rule. 224 pp. Luminous,
complex novel of interrelationships.　　ISBN 0-930044-48-7　　8.95

These are just a few of the many Naiad Press titles — we are the oldest and largest lesbian/feminist publishing company in the world. We also offer an enormous selection of lesbian video products. Please request a complete catalog. We offer personal service; we encourage and welcome direct mail orders from individuals who have limited access to bookstores carrying our publications.